To Mom and Dad

Fool in Love

1

There is a bald man of fifty-nine that spends his days sitting alone only a block from the old barbershop on Parsons Street. He asks for spare change and tells jokes to those that will take the time to listen. His mother used to call him Henry Alexander years ago when he was still her little boy. To his childhood friends he was always Henny. His father would call him son or nothing at all, and his brother just cursed at him most of the time. Nowadays, the people of the city know him as Curly, which he doesn't mind much as it's only out of jest and better than when they call him a bum.

He knows he isn't the most put together man. There's dirt deep within his pores and clumped under his nails, and there are calluses along the sides of his feet from all the nights spent under the rain. Then, of course, there's the crook in his nose from when he ran headfirst into the family swing set. He was only six then, out in the backyard with his brother, James, pretending to be fighter planes. It's with fondness that he remembers himself standing in front of the mirror with those two black eyes. There are stains on his leather coat, too, permanently discolored after years of going unwashed. Once his father's, it has become Henry's most prized possession. Holes run along the legs of his faded jeans. His face has aged significantly over the years, unkempt with a patchy, gray beard that grows along his jawline and down his neck.

But these are all flaws he has come to accept as the years have gone by. Superficial and unimportant. It's him. Because despite it all, having lived three years on the streets, he knows he has been the man his father always dreamt of him becoming. Kind and strong, well-mannered. Accepting. So to call him a bum is quite unfair, he thinks, because for a bum to be a bum, the bum must be unhappy with himself to even be considered a bum at all.

Of course, it would be a slight exaggeration to say he is always happy being on the streets. With all the people that smile at him and toss a few cents into his cup, or even just pass by with indifference, come those that can't resist their strange urges to say something to him. He might be used to it by now, but he'll never understand where this abuse stems from. He's been spit and pissed on, sworn at with every word in the book, told to get a job or to move out of the way or to kill himself; he's been beaten as he sat defenseless, treated as if he was no more than dirt.

And there are the days where the weather

simply refuses to coexist with him. He has known more cold nights than warm ones, unable to sleep because of the shivering. He knows, too, what it's like trying to stay dry from beneath the cover of overhangs or cardboard boxes barely big enough to cover his head, the rain pounding upon him with an unforgiving fury. Even worse are the days the sun beats down upon the city, the air stiflingly humid, shade but a hidden treasure.

The chiming of bells stirs him. The glass door of the diner swings open. A brown-haired girl, looking not much older than a teenager, pokes her head out. She smiles down at him, all the while wiping her hands against her white apron. "Why don't you come in here and get warm for a while?"

"Oh, no, I'm fine," he says with a smile. "It's starting to warm up again, I think."

Her voice is gentle, but unmoving. "I've seen you out here all week. Please come inside, at least for a little while. Won't you?"

"I might just do that," Henry says. "Thank you."

Her face disappears back inside, and he sits for a moment still staring at where she stood. His father raised him an honest man, one that would work the hard way rather than the easy. Even if those around him were taking shortcuts, he was to carry on as he always had. But, his father also didn't raise him to be stupid. As a particularly cold gust of wind passes down his spine, he slowly rises onto his old legs and steps into the diner as the bells chime again.

It's getting close to eleven now and the place is moving into its usual lull between breakfast and lunch. Taking the booth closest to the door, he looks around and sees only the girl that invited him in and an older lady sitting alone by the back window. It smells faintly of maple syrup and hot coffee, and the sizzling of a grill fills the otherwise silent room. There's a warmness about the place, and he can feel his muscles beginning to relax. A lethargic haven away from the city ticking on outside.

It reminds him of home. On Sunday mornings ages ago, he would wake up to the smells of pancakes and sausage coming from the kitchen. The memory has stuck with him, remembered so vividly it could be placed within the borders of a picture frame. There was always the sound of his father's Sinatra record filling the house; the soulful voice singing of flying away somewhere. Out on the lawn James would play with the dog, and the cacophony of barking and laughter still reminds him how soft the grass was along the soles of his feet. Mother would smile at him in the kitchen as she cooked; she would tell him he's looking more and more like his father with each passing day. She would kiss him on the forehead.

"Oh, good, you've finally come in," the girl says, drawing him back to the present. "I'll get a plate of eggs cooking in the kitchen for you right away. How do you take them?"

"Over-easy, please," he says. "You're much too kind."

"They'll be out in a minute or two, okay?"

"I can't help but ask, your accent – you're not from around here, are you?"

She laughs. "You have a good ear. I've only been in the city a few weeks."

"Where do you come from?"

"I used to live out in the countryside, around Seneca. I'm not sure you'd know where that is."

"I'm not sure I would, either," he admits. "And do you like it? The city, I mean."

"I'm not sure yet. There hasn't been much time to take it all in just yet," she says. "I've really just been trying to get used to it all."

"I'm sure the cold hasn't helped sway your opinion much," he answers with a wry smile.

"Not at all. How can you possibly survive on days like this? There must be somewhere you can stay, for the night at least, out of the cold."

"I haven't had much luck with shelters and things like that over the years, and it's hard to keep looking as I get older. These legs aren't what they used to be," he says.

"No one should have to be out there in this cold."

"It's not so bad. After a while you start going numb and don't feel a thing. Bliss, really," he says with a raspy laugh.

She shakes her head at him and turns away from the table. She goes to take the empty plate of the woman in the corner. The woman smiles up at her, and says that the food was delicious. The best breakfast she has had in years. Her wispy gray hair goes down only to her shoulders, swaying with every movement as she pulls out her wallet.

Outside, the sirens of a police car grow closer and traffic sits at a standstill waiting for it to pass. The sun is masked entirely by the clouds now, and it gives the day a feeling of dullness. Unsaturated, gloomy.

Henry knew his family never had a lot of money. It's just something a kid knows; like how they can always know when their mother is upset or that they've done something wrong. He remembers the new clothes some of the boys at school would wear, and all the new toys they'd tell him they had, and those stories they'd tell of the many vacations they'd been on. They had a lot of things, he realizes now. It was their things that had made him jealous beyond belief. But with his father's business going through the ups and downs that all businesses run into sooner or later, and with his mother out of work, and with James and him needing their school supplies and their baseballs bats and their gloves, he understood money was tight.

Still, his father always treated the family when he could. There would be the mornings he'd wake up his two boys and have them out the door before their mother could protest. The three of them must've been quite the sight, Henry imagines, he and his brother still in their plaid pajama pants. They'd be side-by-side, just behind their father, wearing the jeans he wore every day. And he would lead them into a diner much like this one. His order always just a coffee, but his sons could order whatever they wanted. He never said otherwise, as tight as money was.

The woman sets a plate of eggs and home fries down in front of him. "Here you are."

Henry's eyes grow wide. An eagerness overcomes him; one he hadn't felt since the days he was sitting across from his father at the diner. The eggs are creamy mixtures of yellow and white. Scattered beside are the home fries, cooked to a light crisp, steam drifting from them. It's needless to say his mouth waters from their smells, which go together in perfect tandem. "Are you sure it's all right?"

She smiles at him. "Don't be silly. Eat."

This is all the encouragement he needs. It has been months since he'd seen a warm meal as thoughtfully put together and fresh as this. His hand struggles with unwrapping the fork from the napkin, clumsy in his eagerness. He pulls at it, ripping the paper with his hands. The paper tears open and the fork comes crashing down onto his lap, along with the knife and spoon inside. She laughs at him from across the diner, and shouts something at him that he doesn't hear.

He eats the food just as ravenously, uncaring to the way it looks. The eggs quickly thin out, the bottom of the plate screeching with every wild pass of his fork. His hand goes for the ketchup, and soon his plate is splattered with streaks of red. His attention shifts to the home fries, approaching them with the same energy. Every now and then between bites he'll wash everything down with a sip of coffee, but never does he rest. It all tastes too good to stop even for a moment, really.

Henry believes the chef in the back of the diner must very well be the best cook in the entirety of the city. The food tastes absolutely exquisite, though he feels remorseful to finish. Not only because it's all gone, but also because he must've looked like an animal. His cheeks flush, realizing now how abrasive that was. But it's hard to blame a man that has lived off the pennies of strangers for months. He pushes all the crumbs he's left on the table into a pile with his hand, and slides them off the side of the table into his napkin.

The brown-haired waitress stands over him again, looking at him with a kind look of insistence. "Can I get you something else? Please, I can tell you're hungry."

He waves his hand at her and wipes his mouth with a napkin. "Thank you, but no, I can't accept anything else. Really, I shouldn't."

Her hands go to her hips. "And why not?"

"It's the diet I'm on, you see. Can't be having too many carbs like this."

"Oh, please. Let me get you another plate of eggs."

"Thank you, but you've been much too kind to a man like me already."

She smiles at this. "It's really no trouble at all."

"May I ask, what is your name?"

"Maria," she answers.

"A beautiful name. I had a girlfriend named Maria, you know. I always tell myself she was the one that got away. She was just as beautiful as you are."

"Is that right?"

A laugh. "I'm kidding. But it's a name I'm fond of, anyway, given it's yours."

She laughs, too. "Well, what should I call you then?"

"Most people around here call me Curly. You can, too, if that suits you."

"Curly?" She shakes her head. "Surely you prefer going by something else."

His face lights up with an excitement its withered skin hasn't felt in years. "I didn't think anyone would care to ever ask me that again. You've really made my week, Maria. Henry, you can call me that if you'd like."

"Henry it is, then." She puts her tongue in her cheek. "I have an Uncle named Henry, you know."

"Oh, do you? Might you be lying, too?"

She laughs again. "I really do, actually, though I don't talk to him much. The last time I saw him was Thanksgiving two years ago, and he drank so much before dinner he ended up sleeping right through it."

"Everyone celebrates the holidays differently, I suppose," he says.

"Maybe you're right. I'll be right back with another cup of coffee for you, Henry."

He holds up the mug. "But I'm not even done with my first yet."

Her hands go to her hips. "Please. No one has just one cup of coffee."

At that, she turns and heads away. Out of the

corner of his eye, he sees the woman at the other booth beginning to pull on her coat. She smiles as they meet eyes, and carries on. There is something appealing about her that Henry can't quite put his finger on. There's just a simplicity to her beauty, maybe. The red coat she pulls on matches the little shoes on her feet to perfection. Then a small, gray beanie goes over her hair, every piece where it should be, and she takes her leather purse from the booth and walks for the door.

Any man can get any woman, his father taught him, as long as they have the confidence to do so. His old man spoke with such bravado and care when telling his son this that Henry himself began to believe it. His father would never soften his words when he spoke, telling the little boy he would grow up to be as stocky and peculiar-looking as he was and there wasn't a damn thing he could about that. Your looks won't get you anywhere, his father had said, but it'll be that humor and that charm of yours that will prove more than enough. His father had winked at him, then looked back at his mother in the kitchen and said with a raised voice, how do you think I got to marry a woman as beautiful as your mother?

Ego aside, Henry knew his father spoke with the best of intentions. His father taught him that courting a woman was to be like an argument of

2

sorts, and the man was to evoke something within that woman to give them a chance, or to try, at the very least. Arguments often proved fruitless, of course, but to be left fruitless meant to have made an effort to begin with. Being rejected is nothing to hang your head at, his father had said.

Maria returns with a fresh cup of coffee, steam billowing from its top. "Have you lived in the city your whole life?"

"As long as I can remember, yes. It's been good to me, and I'm grateful for it all. I'll always be here. You can count on that."

Maria raises her eyebrows. "Grateful? For being out there in the cold?"

He chuckles. "It sounds silly, I know. But, I'm happy. I'm not sick. I've seen friends of mine get sick, and they've suffered and I've lost them. Being alive is enough, isn't it? For me, at least."

"I guess I can agree with that," she says.

He smiles at her. "I can see you don't buy it."

"Oh, I don't know. I think it's a nice thought, really."

"But, you think it's silly?"

"Not silly, no. But don't you ever find yourself wanting more?"

"Every now and then, yes. I think everyone wishes for things. But, it'd be silly of me to let myself really want the things I know I can't afford. It's a better use of my time to enjoy the little I've got."

She leans against the side of the booth. "I hope you don't mind me asking you this, but when did you decide it was enough?"

"There's a lot to the story, and it's more than maybe I can tell today, and maybe more than you'd care to hear. But, it goes back to this: my father ran a business that he loved more than anything. Fixing up cars and all that comes with that. He had me working for him in the summers when school was out. I'd do these odd jobs here and there, but nothing big. Then he passed and none of us had expected it. It hit my brother and I differently. He ended up distancing himself, and I don't blame him for that. But I decided I owed it to my father to try and keep the business going. Being there, in a way, helped me grieve with it. Made me feel like a piece of him was still there with me."

"I'm sure that would've made him so proud of you," she says.

"Thank you for saying that. I think it would've, too. I like to think he looks down on me with a smile, even though it didn't last long. I did my best, and I do my best to live as he did, even like this."

"I'm sorry, Henry," she says. "I'm sure he does."

"That was years ago. It's all right. I've run out

of places to go for work, but I've got the city to keep me company. And that's enough."

"You've stopped looking?"

"Things move so fast these days that finding my feet feels like an impossible task. Sometimes I run into people like you that'll humor some old geezer like me and listen for a while, and that's what keeps me going."

She smiles. "My pleasure. It's been a while since I've talked to anyone like this."

Henry shakes his head. "The people in this city don't usually have the time to talk, sadly. There's too much to do, it would seem."

"Oh, I know what you mean," she says. "It's easy to get caught up in it all sometimes."

"Time can be a cruel thing," he says.

She turns and looks behind her. "I should really get to cleaning some of these tables. Is there something else I can get you? Anything at all. Just ask."

"I think I'm all right for now," he says. "Thank you, Maria."

He rests his fork on the plate, and turns to look out the window. A few flakes have begun to fall on the city. Weightless in the wind, each with a unique, gentle chiseling. It's almost disheartening to see them touch the ground; so soon will they be trampled under the boots of a city no longer relishing in the beauty of it all.

Beauty, you see, is a thing of the past.

2

And the girl from the country steps out of a cab
and smiles. The fingers of the wind toy with her
brown hair and gently play with the black dress she
wears only on special occasions like tonight. Around
her, the streetlights give a subtle glow to the falling
snow and the city flows into the night full steam
ahead. The sidewalk itself has a pulse; people pass
her in a hurry, their light chatter bringing the brisk air
to life. Their stories intertwining but only for a
second.

She likes the noise of it all, the city, even if it
still feels unnatural to her. She had been thinking
about it since morning when Curly had asked. It's
certainly new to her; the closeness and energy of it all
are such different strokes from the sheltered, quaint
life she was so used to with her parents, yet she finds
herself beginning to like the change more than she
ever anticipated. She loved the rural life of home, and
it seemed impossible she'd ever leave it behind. Every
face familiar and friendly, she knew the streets inside
and out, and things were always so simple. There is
comfort in simple, and in feeling so protected.
Someone like Henry would never be left on the curb

at home. Someone like Henry would be offered a place to stay for the night, helped to get back on their feet, to find work again.

Yet since she was a little girl she has yearned for adventure and fantasized of worlds out of her reach. They were only daydreams, of course, but they brought her so much joy by simply existing in her head. It's with sincere fondness that she remembers the summer afternoons her little sister and herself spent running through New York City and Paris and London, the grass in their backyard becoming so much more through their little eyes.

They were but kids with imaginations then, and these days those places feel so much less daunting and exciting because they aren't distant any longer. She made it to the city, and the business meetings she'd reenact with her sister became realities hidden only by the walls of skyscrapers. Behind each window are those daydreams, so within her reach that they've become almost worryingly tangible. She really has left home and her parents and all she knew behind. It's something that excites her, and at the same time scares her to no end.

But, with growing up comes change, and she feels this risk is one she has to take to truly find herself.

Maria turns back to find that her cab has

already driven off, and she spins in a circle until she finds Tom through the crowd. He's signaling for her to hurry up, and she shakes her head back. "You're always in such a rush," she says when she gets to him.

"You know how I get when we're late."

He pulls her onward by the arm, fighting his way into the restaurant through drunken people, too busy falling in lust with people they've known only for the night to care of anything else. Waiters and waitresses rush by, sweating in the stale air, hoping for time to pass just a little faster. White tablecloths and wine glasses cover the tables with a façade of elegance. It's a big room, certainly a grand one, but with all the people squeezed into it, the intended class is overshadowed by a damning feeling of claustrophobia. Tom says something to Maria, and she sees his lips move with the words, but his voice is lost somewhere in the bedlam of it all and she simply smiles back to appease him.

A voice from somewhere in the place calls out to Tom, catches his attention somehow, draws him in. He keeps hold of her hand, and takes a few steps toward it, saying something back. To Maria, all of the voices sound as if she were underwater, drowning, awaiting her rescue. She keeps a sheepish smile on her face, knowing Tom might very well be introducing her to another friend he barely recognizes, and one she'd soon forget. There's a crashing of plates from behind her, and she jumps, though she may very well have been the only person in the restaurant to have reacted, to have even noticed. The woman leading them to their table taps her foot, looks at her nails, loses the smile from her face. Maria can see Tom waves goodbye in her daze, and they soon are carrying on through the restaurant, passing more tables. All the while she hopes no one else will call Tom's name, that they'll make it.

At last, the woman holds out her hand to a table, smiling again. They are as far away from the front of the restaurant as they possibly could be, but Maria doesn't notice nor care. Her eyes are focused only on getting into the seat. Tom, however, sighs as they sit and makes a point of asking the woman seating them if there is any other table they could have. There aren't.

"They must not want anyone seeing us," Tom says with a laugh. "Is this all right?"

"It's perfect," she answers meekly. Her hands are sweating, and she wipes them against her dress as she tries to catch her breath. It all feels a bit dizzying, being shepherded through all those people to simply eat dinner. She knows Tom likes to eat out – it's what he grew up doing. He has been bred for this climate.

Maria looks at him across the table, busy

scanning over the menu, unfazed. She clears her throat, doing her best to find a sense of composure and cool herself down. "Get a lot of work done today?"

"You know I never do," he says, running his hands through his hair like he always does. It barely moves with all the gel he puts into it. "The day I can leave will be the best day of my life."

"At least you don't have to wash any tables at your job," she says, forcing a laugh.

He squints. "You like it so far, though, don't you?"

"No complaints here," she answers. "It's been pretty easy-going so far. After the rush it's just a lot of watching the clock and waiting to go home."

He sits back and pulls a pack of cigarettes from his pocket. "Slacking on the job?"

"You caught me," she says with a genuine laugh. "But I do like it, don't think I don't."

He puts a cigarette in his mouth and lights it before answering. "And they're treating you well?"

"Better than at any other job I've worked. I think some of them are just glad to have a new face around."

"A pretty face, at that," he tells her with a smile. "You look great in that dress, you know."

She looks down at it, judging for herself. "I

wear this too much, don't I?"

He taps the cigarette against his glass. "Maria, I wouldn't mind if you wore it every day."

"It would start to stink, Tom," she says, her eyes scanning the menu. "We really should've went somewhere cheaper, though. You can't keep treating me like this."

"It isn't that much," he says, as he does every time he takes her out. "If you'd rather somewhere else there's still time to sneak out of here."

She pretends to ready herself to go. "Fine, but I'll tell you now I can't run very fast in these heels."

"You're getting left behind, then," he says.

Maria's eyes grow as the waiter appears. "Quiet, quiet, he'll hear our plan."

They wait as they are each poured a glass of wine. An older couple at the table next to theirs stands to leave. The woman pulls a thick, red headband over her light, blonde hair. Outside, the snowfall grows thicker. Maria smiles at the waiter as he turns to go.

Tom leans forward against the table, his hands folded on top of it. "So, what about school? Have you thought anymore about it?"

A frown. One that feels familiar. "Really?"

He sighs at her. "You know I like to ask."

"It's every night, Tom. I'm sick of talking about

this."

"Maria, you never give me an answer," he snaps.

She rubs her hands against her dress. "This isn't the right time for this."

"Will there ever really be a right time? Because lately there hasn't been and it's getting a little old always waiting to know," he says, the cigarette smoke dancing in the air.

She studies his eyes, full of fire. "I don't know. I'm not at the point in my life where I know for sure what to pursue."

He persists. "What things would have to change? I'm sure we can fix them."

"I'm still getting settled in," she says. "It's been a big change for me."

"What has? Being here?"

"The city, all these people. Living with you. It's a lot," she says.

"I know it is, Maria. But you're a smart girl –"

He stops his words short, feeling the presence of their waiter above them. He stares down at them, a smile plastered across his face. "Ready to order?"

"I'll have the tortellini, please," Maria says, doing her best to sound lighthearted.

"The rabbit for me." He puts the cigarette back in his mouth.

The waiter leaves them there in a tense quiet, though the restaurant screams with life. The clicking of forks, the sound of laughter, the echoing of voices. Maria keeps quiet, looking across the table at Tom. He keeps his eyes away from her. She's unbothered by a few moments of silence, happy to wait for him to speak.

Out the window is the woman with the red headband. The woman's date holds an umbrella over her head and holds a hand out to the street. The woman is clutching the man's arm and retelling a story in his ear. She speaks with great enthusiasm, not even pausing as they get into the cab. It quickly drives off, smoke dancing out from the back of it and twirling into the night. The car goes to the end of the street and takes a right. The thin apartment buildings along the roads show signs of the season – lit by red and green and white bulbs, garnished with wreaths, and every now and then there are little glimpses of trees through the thin glass of a window. They stop at a red light, and the woman takes her date's hand in hers with a smile and a sigh of blissful joy. Her eyes go out the window to a homeless man resting with his back against the foundation of the tunnel.

Henry looks back at her, but she quickly turns away. He pulls a blanket up higher on his neck. Cars pass above, feet march through snow, distant music drifts by. Fridays are always the loudest, and it's only amplified by the holiday. Usually he'd be out there asking for change, taking in all the sights, wishing people a good Christmas, but the wind is much too wicked for that tonight.

The light changes and the cab heads onward into the dark. The woman remembers something else, another part of the story, and goes back into it. Perhaps this story would follow them into their bed, into their dreams. Perhaps not.

Tom looks back to her, finally. "I trust you to make the right choices for yourself, Maria. It's just important to me."

"I know," she answers, forcing a smile.

"You haven't even touched your drink," he says.

"I'm not really in the mood for wine tonight," Maria tells him. "Maybe in a little while."

A half-smile. "That's not like you."

A shrug. "Maybe I'm changing."

"I like you the way you are already."

She rolls her eyes, though her shoulders relax a bit. "I met someone today at work, you know."

A raise of his eyebrows. "Was he better looking than me?"

Maria laughs. "His name is Henry. He's homeless, so he's always out there in the cold when

I'm working. I've seen him a few times now and it's so hard to let him waste away when we have so much extra food in the kitchen. Today I cracked and invited him inside."

He holds his cigarette between his fingers. "And he came in?"

"He would've been crazy not to," she says. "I think it was good for him. He seemed happy with it. Happy to have someone to talk to for a while."

"And he's homeless, you said?"

"Yes. But you wouldn't be able to tell from talking with him." She smiles as she says this. "He has such a funny, little personality about him."

Tom laughs. "Sounds like you made yourself a friend."

"Oh, I don't know," she says. "I don't know if he'll want to come back in. He seemed to feel terrible about it taking so much."

Their waiter brings their food to the table now. He places a lavish plate of rabbit served on top of white polenta with figs and green olives in front of Tom. The tortellini stuffed with scallops and crabmeat, served on top of a tomato and coriander paste goes in front of Maria. He cups his hands together and smiles at them. The aromas of the fresh plates waft together and produce a truly delectable smell. "Can I get anything else for you two?"

"No, thank you," Tom answers. He stuffs his cigarette out against the table and leans forward. "David told me to get this, so it better be good."

Maria squints. "David?"

"You know him, I think. My friend from work. He has the little girl with him."

She thinks for a second, a fork waiting in her hand. "Oh, I don't know. You have so many friends."

Tom laughs as he cuts into his meal. "I don't blame you for forgetting. They're all so similar."

3

David curses as he slams the door shut, finally finding shelter from the bite of the wind. It can be a bitch come wintertime. Every light in the house is out, and the only noise is the ticking of the grandfather clock from the living room. "Lynn?"

From upstairs comes a giggle, followed by the rapid succession of feet on wooden stair-steps. He turns on the lights and slides down to the floor. The sleepy face of a brown-haired little girl rounds the corner, her cheeks curling into a smile when she sees him sitting there.

"Daddy!" She runs to his arms and he pulls his daughter in close. She screams as they embrace. "Oh, gross! You're all wet!"

He laughs into her hair and clutches tighter as she squirms. "It's just the snow," he says. "Shouldn't you be asleep?"

"I was waiting for you to come home and tuck me in."

He looks past her into the kitchen. "When did Julia leave?"

"An hour ago," she says. "She said she didn't want to get stuck in the snow."   "Smart girl. Sorry

I'm so late. There was traffic."

Lynn gives him a look of concern. "Is there a lot of snow, Daddy?"

"There's plenty," he says.

"Will we be snowed in?"

"The plows will come. There isn't enough for that."

"You smell funny, Daddy," she tells him.

He pushes her head away from his jacket. "So everything was all right when you were here all by yourself?"

She looks away. "Yes, I guess so."

"Did something happen?"

Her body begins to twist at the waist, rocking back and forth with the shaking of her little head. "I don't think I want to say."

David smiles at her. "I won't be mad, Lynn. You can tell me."

She sighs, and stares guiltily down at her feet. "I got scared and I called mommy."

He slides lower down the wall. "You did?"

"I know you told me not to, daddy. I didn't mean to. But I heard something downstairs. I'm sorry."

"Don't be sorry." He kisses her on the forehead. "It was my fault."

"I shouldn't have called her."

"If you were scared you did the right thing. Did she say anything?"

"Just that she misses me," she says. "And that she wants me to come home soon."

David runs his hand along his daughter's cheek. "Look, why don't you head upstairs? I'll be right behind you."

She looks into his eyes. "Will you tell me a story?"

"Only if you're good," he says.

She smiles and jumps off him, running back upstairs as quickly as she came down. David gets himself up off the floor on unsure legs, taking his time to move away from the wall. His eyes feel tired, the world around him spinning, and as he goes to the kitchen he does his best to rub the sleep away.

He tries never to get upset with Lynn, like his father always used to with him. It isn't fair to be upset with a child for being scared, and David knows this. But Shannon gets so worried when their daughter stays with him and he'd rather her not have another reason to curse him out. He loved that woman when they were together, and he loves her now, but damn, can she yell.

Shannon gave him Lynn by accident – an accident that haunted him every night as the due date inched closer. Barely grown into a man, and now carelessly falling into the role of father. But then he was holding their baby girl in his arms for the first time. She was only four goddamn pounds, staring up at him from within his big hands with these little, blue eyes as fulfilling as the early morning sea. The little tuft of blonde hairs on her head, the toothless mouth, peaceful while being held by her father.

That tiny thing with the little, blue eyes became the first person to show him how tangible love can be.

Out the back window of the kitchen and through the dark he can see the oak tree in the middle of the yard. The one Shannon had laid beneath, reading Lynn stories as he made them dinner. The nights they spent drunk together laughing about college and friends and the future. He really does wish she didn't have to grow up sharing time between her parents. That it could've worked. That he'd been stronger.

About a year ago is when he told her he couldn't keep doing it. She was the same girl, with the dimples on her cheeks and her brown eyes, oversized and bright. Things were how they'd always been until that honeymoon phase of being young and free started to flicker out. Things started hitting him hard, pushing him towards a feeling of being trapped. All of a sudden they had a house to tend to and jobs to get to and a little girl to raise. Their time of naïve indifference together had run out, and he felt himself overwhelmed by it all. Dropped into adulthood, unprepared and afraid.

He blinks, and his eyes lose focus of the tree. The window becomes enveloped in blackness, his reflection now staring back at him. He looks a lot like his own father these days; the broad shoulders, the receding brown hair streaked with grays, the long nose. The tired eyes, traced with deep, purple rings.

Turning away, he heads up the staircase and past the picture frames hung on the wall. Too dark to see tonight. He knocks on Lynn's bedroom door and goes to her bedside. Her green sleeping light shines across her cheek, keeping her safe from the ghosts in her closet. She giggles as he kicks one of her dolls across the hardwood floor.

"Barbie might have a black eye in the morning," David says.

"That's okay," she tells him. "I'm sure Santa will bring me a new one."

David closes his eyes and takes a deep breath. "How long is it until Christmas?"

"Two days, Daddy," she says, practically squealing in excitement. "You should know that!"

He rubs his palms together. "You'll be at your mom's for it?"

Lynn waits to answer for a moment. "She said

she's taking me to Nana's. Is that okay with you?"

He sits beside her on the bed. "As long as you're happy about it, yes."

"But Daddy, I want you to be happy."

"Are you excited to be seeing your Nana?"

"Yes," she says. "I love my Nana."

"Then I'm happy, too."

"They don't want you to come, do they?"

"It's not that they wouldn't let me," David says. "I think it's just better that I don't."

Lynn pulls her blanket up to her chin. "Daddy?"

"Yes?"

"Are you sad because mommy moved away?"

"No," he says softly. He does his best to smile. "It was what was best for you, Lynn."

"But was it what you wanted, Daddy?"

He sighs, and looks over at the doorway. "I think it's time for bed. Okay?"

She frowns, her face entirely transparent in showing the pain she feels. "I don't want to leave you."

David squeezes his daughter's shoulder. "We still get to have breakfast together in the morning."

"I like having breakfast with you," she says, but her expression stays the same.

"What should we have?"

"Daddy, I want you to pick. You never get to pick."

David smiles at this. "Are you sure?"

"Yes, Daddy!"

"Hmm… this is hard," he says. "I'm not so sure I like being the one to choose."

She bounces in the bed. "What do you like?"

"A lot of different stuff," he says with a smile. "You know your daddy likes to eat."

Her excitement becomes impatience. "Just tell me your favorite food!"

"I don't think we should be having pizza for breakfast"

Lynn giggles at this. "No, daddy! Breakfast foods only. What is your favorite breakfast food?"

A laugh. "Well, you should've said that in the first place. Hmm, let's see… why don't we make chocolate chip pancakes?"

"Are those your favorite, daddy?"

"Yes," he says.

She smiles. "Okay."

"Okay. Goodnight, Lynn."

"Daddy, wait. You promised you'd tell me a story, remember?"

"Oh, right. Of course."

"Do you have one to tell me?"

"I do. It's about chocolate chip pancakes."

"They're your favorite."

"Before you had me as your daddy, I had my very own daddy. He would've been your grandpa if you two ever met."

"Did he die, daddy?"

"No, he didn't die. We don't talk much anymore, though."

She furrows her eyebrows. "He's your daddy and you don't talk?"

"He didn't like some of the things I did in my life, and I told him he could go to hell for all I cared. But you don't need to hear about that. Never tell your daddy to go to hell, okay? It's not very nice."

"You made me promise to never swear, Daddy. I wouldn't."

"That's my girl. But, look. I'm sure your grandpa would love you as much as I do if he ever met you."

"Does he want to meet me?"

"I don't know. You have to understand that he grew up in a different time than me and you. Some of his beliefs are a little more serious than maybe they should be."

"Do you believe in them, too?"

"No, I don't. I think they're stupid."

"I believe in what you believe, daddy."

"But I'm not telling you that he was a bad man.

Remember that, all right? It was the way he was raised. I still do have some fond memories of him."

"Like pancakes?"

"Exactly. He used to make pancakes for me while I watched cartoons every Saturday morning with my brother. You know my brother as Uncle PJ, don't you?"

"He's the funniest uncle I've got," she says with a giggle.

"That's right. My daddy would make us those pancakes, and they were the best damn pancakes you'd ever eat. He made them into these little, tiny circles. As tiny as you are."

"I'm not that tiny, Daddy. Mommy says I'm getting big."

"You are. I guess you could think of them like really thin, soft, chocolatey hockey pucks."

"You can't eat hockey pucks, Daddy," she says smugly.

He laughs. "These ones you could eat without getting sick, I promise. Unless you ate too many. I swear they taste better when they're small like that. See, if you make them too big they'll dry out too much and there won't be enough chocolate chips in each one. With the little ones, there's something in every bite."

"You're making me hungry, daddy. You'll

make the little ones for me, won't you?"

"I wouldn't dare make them any other way. My daddy was the best cook."

She yawns and blinks away sleep. "Do you miss him, Daddy?"

"I miss a lot of people. But that's all part of growing up. I just have to get used to that."

She touches his big hand with her little one. "You don't have to miss me, Daddy. I'll always come back to you no matter what."

He smiles. "I know you will."

"Will you always be here for me, Daddy?"

"Always. No matter how long it takes you to come back. I'll be waiting."

"Good," she whispers.

"Sweet dreams," David says.

"Goodnight, Daddy."

He stays sitting there with her, softly drawing lines in her back with his fingernails, letting himself absorb the precious time he has with her. His fingers loop around in circles, drawing eights over and over. Easing her into her dreams. If only infinity weren't so far out of his reach.

Lynn's bedroom walls are adorned with her art, a gallery of years gone by. Shan had always pushed her to color, even when she was still missing her front teeth and any words to speak. It's easy to find drawings from that year – they aren't much more than wild strips of color. She was a maniac with the crayons as a baby, thrashing her hands across page after page of paper. David would always sit and watch her go, telling each and every one was a masterpiece. As his eyes move across the walls, he can see gradual improvement – the chaos has begun to resemble people, or animals, cars, trees, birds. There's even one of him, a block head with brown hair and big, red lips. Of course, he could only tell because across the top she wrote 'Daddy' with a backwards 'y' in green.

Lynn's breathing has slowed. Knowing she's fast asleep, he gets himself up off the bed and slowly goes over to the door. Looking back one last time, he can't seem to find her face in the dark.

4

The day after a snowfall is always the worst for Henry. Everything is so wet. Powdered white falls from rooftops with the passing of wind. Sidewalks become a dirty mess of slush and shoe bottoms. Ice awaits around every corner, always where he least expects, and he knows these sudden jumps of his heart will end up killing him someday.

He finds solace in the warmth of the diner again, as much as his father would disapprove of his coming back a second time. He feels he's beginning to soften with each year that goes by. The black, leather coat he wears may have been warm twenty years ago when his father first bought it, but these days, more than anything else, it's just something to wear.

Across the diner, a young mother with blonde hair reads the menu out loud for her little boy. They sit on the same side of a booth, and he looks up at her with the utmost attention. So full of unbridled energy for life. His face brightens at each new choice his mother reads; waffles, pancakes, omelets, home fries.

The small eyes are what always get Henry. They long to learn, and he knows he has a lot he could teach. Being a father was never really an opportunity he got to pursue. In his younger years, he was too shy to ever dance with any of the girls like his friends did. When he started to work, this took up so much of his time that he put off even thinking about finding a wife. He told himself he'd get to it. That never quite panned out.

Maria goes over to the little boy and the Ma and asks if they're ready to order. The boy looks her in the eyes and tells her he is. "What will it be?" she asks.

There had been one woman. Her name was Camille, and she's the only girl he's ever been with. He remembers thinking the name was absolutely repulsive back when they went to high school together. Now he finds it charming, actually, for whatever reason. Maybe from the nostalgia of it. The name fit her perfectly, in hindsight. She was tall -- much taller than him. So tall, in fact, that he felt too embarrassed standing beside her to allow himself to be seen with her. God, does that sound stupid to him now. They would only ever talk at parties on the weekends, when they would both drink a little too much and his inhibitions were forgotten. This talking slowly became more, as this type of thing often did, and every time he would wake up the next morning and tell himself that would be the last time. She was a nice enough girl, and he liked it, of course, but his father raised him an honest boy. He would have to end it with her.

Life, however, has a funny way of working itself out. Come graduation, Camille told him one night as they lay on opposite sides of the bed that she would be moving away. With some other boy, as it turns out. She would be going west. To California. That's where everyone's going, she told him that night, and he believed her. I think we both know what this was, she had said, and he had nodded. He wished her the best of luck with all she did with her life, and left. He hasn't seen her since, except for in his dreams from time to time on particularly lonely nights. She never does age, that Camille, though the details of her face have faded since.

Maria places a plate of two, big, chocolate chip pancakes, one on top of the other, in front of the boy. His face brightens up in an instant.

The bell atop the door rings. Henry has his back to the door, but hears a woman's voice greet Maria from across the diner. She asks for just one menu. They soon pass by his table, Maria in her white smock and jeans followed by the woman in the red coat from yesterday. They go to a little table in the middle of the restaurant. The woman sits, takes off the coat and hangs on the edge of the booth, and asks for a coffee.

Such elegance. She really is beautiful, and Henry can't help but stare. Even from a distance he can see the intricacies of her face; little dimples carved into her cheeks, a soft smile persistent on her lips.

"How are the eggs, sir?"

He jumps from his seat. "My god, you scared me."

Maria laughs at him. "On edge this morning?"

"I was just a little distracted. The eggs are exceptional, thank you."

"Did you get through last night all right? The snow hit pretty hard."

"Oh, it was fine," he says, looking past her. "It certainly could've been worse."

Maria smiles. "I see you watching her, you know. Does someone have a crush?"

"Watching who?" Curly says, his attention going back to Maria.

"Don't play dumb with me."

"Tell me," he says, "I know you've only worked here a few weeks, but do you know who she is? Is she here a lot?"

"Since I've been working here, I've seen her most mornings, now that I think about it."

"I'd like to know her," Henry says.

Maria purses her lips at him. "You'd have to go and introduce yourself then."

"Look at me," he says. "I can't go over there looking like this. Will you?"

"Will I what?"

"Talk to her for me."

Maria laughs at this. "And say what?"

"Ask if she'll be back tomorrow. I need to know."

"That's a lot of responsibility you're putting on me," she says with a smile.

He leans back against the booth and puts his hands over his face. "I'm such a fool and I know it. A fool in love."

"Everyone that falls in love has to be a little foolish. Don't they?"

"Surely a woman like that must be married, though. Or better yet, she knows she's too good for any man to ever get her hand. Especially not me. It would be like a mutt going for a poodle."

"That doesn't even make sense, Henry."

"It gets old being on your own for so long. It really does. Just for one night I'd like not to be by myself."

Maria looks over at the woman. She pulls at her finger. "I didn't see a ring, you know."

Henry leans in closer, and lowers his voice. "You didn't?"

"No," she says, whispering, too. "Lately, I'm

always looking at other women's rings. I would've noticed."

"So you'll talk to her for me?"

"What's in it for me?"

"I don't have much to–"

"Stop," she says with a laugh. "I'm kidding, Henry. Of course I'll talk to her."

"Oh, thank you. You're so kind to an old bum like me."

"Have you even considered what you'll say to her, though?"

This stumps him for a moment, and he squints at her. "What I'll say?"

She laughs. "You know, like where you'll offer to take her on this date?"

Again, a look of bemusement. "Date, you said?"

"Yes, a date, Henry."

"People still go on those these days?"

"We do, Henry. Of course we do. What else would there be to do?"

"Then I suppose I'll take her on a date through the city. It's the thing I know the most about. One of the only things, in all honesty. How to avoid the crowds, the best places to see the lights, things like that. I'd love to show her around. If she would be up for it, of course."

"That sounds lovely. Any woman would love that, I'm sure."

He rubs his chin. "But I can't have her seeing me like this. She'll laugh at me."

"She won't laugh at you. If she gets to know you like I do, she'll agree in a heartbeat."

"She'll pity me. I don't want that. I'm tired of that."

"Why don't I bring you a change of clothes? My boyfriend has plenty. He won't mind at all."

Henry mulls it over, tapping his fork against the side of his plate. "Will she be back, do you think? Tomorrow, I mean."

"I don't see why not," Maria says. "I told you she comes in almost every day. You better pray she isn't sick of this place yet."

"You're sure he won't mind?"

"I'm sure, Henry. But you have to promise me you'll go through with this if I bring you the shirt."

He sighs, and leans his head back against the booth. She stands there smiling down at him, her hands clutched tightly together.

A shake of the head. "Don't go begging now. I'll think about it."

"Promise me, Henry," she says. "Promise me or I'm not bringing the shirt."

"Fine," he says. "I promise."

The last time he made a promise he then vowed never to promise anything to anyone ever again. It was a promise he had no choice to make really – the last inning of a baseball game, he promised his teammates he wouldn't strike out. Their last hope, losing by a run, it was his turn to get up to the plate. Clutching the bat in his hands, tightening his grip to keep himself from shaking, he walked up there with the façade that he'd be the hero they needed.

And of course he struck out; there really was no chance it would go any other way. And of course his teammates blamed him, as they always did. He felt shame for months. Years after, really, as he often sees the same scene replayed in his dreams. Always the same outcome.

He goes to the door of the diner, waving to Maria. She taunts him with reassurance. Faking a smile to match hers, he tries his best to convince himself that tomorrow will go the way he hopes. That he won't faint in front of her, or forget to speak, or turn and run and never look back. Though, despite his hopes, he leaves with a lingering sense of dread.

The traffic moves cautiously through the melting snow, their tires sliding right along through the newly-formed puddles. They deepen with every minute that goes by it seems, the buildings and sidewalks shedding their white coatings. Henry finds himself ducking every now and then to avoid falling droplets of water from streetlights. The day still feels young, and he takes his time breathing in the cool air as he goes along.

Despite his fears of failure, there's a sense of purpose within him. It's one he doesn't often feel, and he holds his head high as he walks through the streets. The woman may reject him, and she may laugh in his face, but like everyone else he has plans for his week. Like everyone else he has a newfound goal and a mission to achieve it. As he rounds a corner, he finds himself smiling. It's reserved but present, a smile that has forced itself up past his doubts, unwilling to leave his face as he continues on his way. People pass him, some indifferent, some nodding, some smiling back.

Henry stops in front of the window of a candy store and scrutinizes his reflection. Next door is the nursing home his mother lives in. He sees his own face in the glass, of course; if he were to see someone else's face he'd worry he was going mad. But upon seeing his own face, there's a rush of contempt for the little details marring its skin. Running his fingers along his chin, he feels the small bumps of zits and unshaven hairs. His cheeks feel almost scaly, like a lizard would feel, he imagines, from the many nights he has laid his head down on a park bench or drywall to sleep. The dark circles around his eyes give him a look of a depraved raccoon, and he curses himself under his breath.

Henry knows these things are all superficial and unimportant, but these are things mothers don't often overlook. To rephrase that, mothers often *can't* overlook these things. It's only natural for a mother to critique every single aspect of their sons and daughters. They do this out of love, the purest form of love there is, really, telling their children they look utterly terrible every chance they get. It's with the best intentions, it's because they want their kids to look their best, to be reflections of themselves. But by God, does it hurt.

He pulls open the door of the nursing home, and steps inside. It smells only of perfume and old roses, a pang of warmth hitting him in the face. It's dark in the room, and he finds his way towards the woman behind a desk as his eyes adjust from the sun. The woman isn't interested in him quite yet, busy instead with the crossword puzzle rested on her lap. He knows her well, actually. She's always the one to greet him when he comes, and there hasn't been a single time that she hasn't been deeply invested in one of those puzzles.

When she does finally look up at him, through

the frames of her wide, brown glasses, he can see the edges of her eyes perk up in recognition. "I was wondering when you'd be back, Henry."

"I know, I'm sorry I haven't been here more often."

What's it been? A few weeks?"

"Maybe two or three now. How has she been doing?"

"She'll been doing great as soon as she sees you, I'm sure," she says, standing and walking past him towards a hallway in the back. "Come with me."

The two of them make their way past a line of doors, each with their own numbers. Each with their own, unique stories waiting to be told inside. All the places travelled, all the love they've felt, all the things they've done. Henry's mother is room 21, he remembers, and he waits as the woman knocks lightly against it.

His mother did her best to keep their old house up and running after his father died, but she never did have the same energy for it. It was a lot for one woman to handle on her own, with her sons out focused on making a living and her age getting up there. Henry always feels guilty about not having helped her more all those years she spent out in the garden under the sun. Money had always been tight, and it only worsened without his father. He feels it was for the best when she finally sold the house and came here. It was a change she may not have wanted, but one she has grown accustomed to. She has friends here, and all their gossip that she loves to talk with him about, and less things to worry over. He knows she misses her boys, though. She must miss the freedom, too.

The door opens, and his mother stands there looking back at him with a tired look in her eyes. She has her hair cut short and the same look of annoyance that has been a constant on her face like she always has. When she sees her son, however, her little boy standing there smiling at her, a light comes over her face. She smiles, and holds her arms out to him.

He shakes a hand at her. "I don't think you want to hug me smelling like this."

She laughs and grabs him by the hand. "Don't be silly, my Henry. I haven't been able to smell anything in years."

He can't help but laugh, too, and he embraces her with reluctance. It had been too long since he had held her. Taking her gently by the arm, leading her over to a brown, leather chair in her room. He takes the chair beside it, and he feels her take his hand in hers.

"You don't come by enough, my Henry," she says, her voice little more than a whisper. "I very much like seeing you."

"I don't like coming when I look like this," he tells her.

"You've always been my handsome son," she says. "You still are."

"Sometimes I forget it," he says. "They're still treating you well, right?"

"I have everything I could possibly need," she says with a nod of her head. "It's not like I need much these days."

"You look great," Henry says.

"No need to lie to your mother," she answers with a laugh. "We aren't looking our best, are we? My skin is so gray, and yours isn't too much better."

"Maybe you're right, Ma."

"You know, you look more and more like your father every time I see you, my Henry," she says, squeezing his hand.

"You tell me that a lot," he says. "I don't know if I see it."

"You two have the same eyes. Always looking around, taking things in. You're very watchful of everything. Since you were a kid you've been doing that. Nothing ever got past you."

Henry smiles. "Dad was like that, too?"

"Oh, you know how your father was," she answers. "He loved people. He couldn't help it. I don't think he ever forgot a face."

"We were lucky to have him," he says.

His mother perks up all of a sudden. She holds up a finger towards him, and turns towards the shelf behind her with eagerness. The shelf is cluttered with stacks of worn books, magazines, and picture frames. As she thumbs through the piles, a cloud of dust takes shape above and a mustiness comes over the room. Henry feels a tickle in his nose, but it doesn't seem to bother her as she goes about searching.

When she turns back to him, she has a thin print between her fingers that she holds out to her son. "I've been meaning to give this to you one of these times."

Henry takes it from her and flips it over to reveal a black and white photograph. It's of him as a little boy, wearing his favorite Superman t-shirt, a wide smile spread across his little face. Beside him is his father, laid back against the sofa with his arm around Henry and his leg crossed over the other. There's a smile on his face, too. The two of them together, their old home in the background with Henry and his brother's toys scattered across the floorboards, the white walls, the familiarity.

The picture shakes in Henry's hand. A colorless snapshot rich with nostalgia and joy, with sincerity, with importance.

5

Maria crosses the street as quickly as she can. The midday traffic is heavier than usual given the influx of those looking to get a head start on their holiday. Her teeth rattle in the cold, but at least the sky is clear of any clouds for once. The sun, yellow and bright and present, reminds her of warmer times, though purely aesthetic today.

Tom's office building is only three blocks from the apartment. It's an engineering company called Kimball's that takes work on buildings, bridges, and roads. Maria really doesn't know that much about it, considering Tom hates talking about work and always finds a way to change the subject if she asks about it. It was never his plan to be an engineer. He had wanted to be a writer, apparently, but his parents vetoed that and sent him away. He likes the money; that's what he always tells her. That it was worth it for the paycheck. She says if he isn't happy that he could still always give up his job and start over. That's where the conversation always ends.

The building is made of brick, faded to a maroon color, and stands so tall she feels anxious looking up at it. Heights have never appealed to her.

Back home, mostly everything stands below three stories. She goes up the two sets of stone steps in the front and pulls open the door.

Another staircase waits inside. The interior is even darker than the streets under the gray sky outside, and for a moment she doubts whether this is really the right place. This is her first time here. Tom told her if she ever needed to talk that she could come straight to his office. I promise you I won't be doing my work, he had told her.

Growing up, Ma and Pa would keep their fights private from her and her sister, but she always knew, nonetheless. Pa is too prideful to ever admit he's wrong, no matter how evident it is; growing up with four brothers will do that to a man. Ma's problem is she simply doesn't listen to his side of the disagreement. She has a one-track mind when it comes to the way she feels. After years together, they've become so methodical in the way they argue. For a few days at a time, Maria will see the two of them barely speak any words to each other, other than to wish each other a good morning and to ask who's cooking dinner. It's them giving each other space, before finally they'll sit down and they'll talk. By then, most of the arguments feel silly and weightless, and they won't even care anymore.

As Maria goes higher up the stairs, the smell of

cigarettes grows stronger. She holds her breath. Back home, her father always seemed to have one clenched between his teeth. She never minded; the smell let her know she was home. Now they just make her miss it.

She comes to a small strip of doors, the hallway covered in a rust-colored carpet and the walls barren except for mail slots. There are gold numbers on the doors, and she slowly makes her down reading them. Tom told her he was '220.'

A week or two after she moved in, he came home from work with a bouquet of flowers for her. The change was really hitting her hard, trying to adapt and learn and find comfort, and he could tell. It was a small thing, but it helped. Those flowers made her feel loved, and they eased the rocking of the boat just enough to help her find her feet.

All of the doors are closed as she goes down the hall. His is near the middle, shut tight. After knocking three or four times, and waiting for a minute, she sighs and turns away.

Down on the far side of the hall, there is a sliver of light coming through the opening of a door. The only open door in the entirety of the building. Going to it, she pushes gently against it. "Excuse me?"

A man looks up from behind a desk. He has a gray jacket slung over his arm, and wears a white, collared shirt with a brown and orange, checkered tie and gray pants. "Yes?"

"I'm sorry, I don't mean to bother you. I was just wondering if you've seen Tom today?"

The man stares up at her for a moment, squinting his eyes. Then his face seems to light up, and he says: "Oh, you must be Maria. Come in, if you'd like."

"Thank you," she says, stepping into the office. "I hope I'm not intruding."

"It's the day before a break, I'm not all that focused on work."

"I'm surprised they even have you in here," she says. "The rest of the office seems like it's dead."

"I figured I'd get some last-minute work in. But Tom left a little while ago, actually. He's out meeting a client for lunch."

Maria frowns. "It's a little late for lunch, isn't it?"

"Clients usually aren't all that flexible. We take whatever time we can get with them."

She stares at his face, analyzing it. "I don't mean to be rude, but which of his friends are you? He's told me a couple names."

"No, don't worry," he answers. "We all look the same around here. I'm David."

"Oh, all right. That would've been my first guess," she says with a laugh. "Do you mind if I wait for him for a little while?"

"Go right ahead. Sit, if you'd like. I'm not sure how soon he'll be back, though."

"That's all right." Maria sits in a chair by his desk, and lets her eyes wander around the office. His desk looks like a storm has just passed through, but Maria likes the messiness. It makes it feel more intimate than workplaces normally do. There are a few picture frames lined around the edges, encircling files and files overflowing with papers. On the left, a model of a red Mustang, and on the right, a stapler, a mug of pens, and a calculator.

"He talks a lot about you, you know," David says.

She gives him a half-smile. "Good things, I hope."

He laughs. "Oh, of course. All good things."

She reaches for one of the frames on his desk, taking it with both hands. She stares intently into the picture, smiling. It's of David and a short woman with blond hair and a little girl in-between the two of them. "Is this your wife?"

"We were never married, actually. But we broke up," he says.

Maria puts it back down on the desk. "And do you miss her?"

He shifts in his seat. "I'm not sure how to answer that."

Concern shows in her eyes. "I'm sorry. It was weird of me to ask."

He shakes his head. "My fault. I should really get rid of that picture."

She frowns. "Well, can you tell me if you're doing all right?"

He sits down on his desk, and rubs his hands against his legs. "I'm getting there. It's a little weird learning how to live on my own again, if that makes sense. But I'm really starting to move past it, I think."

"It does," she answers. "But just because you're moving on doesn't mean you can't be upset, too."

He rubs his hands against his pants again. "It's warm in here, isn't it?"

"Don't change the subject on me," she says to him, crossing her arms.

"I'm starting to sweat."

"Excuse me," she says.

He drops from the desk and goes over to the window of his office, cracking it open a little to let some air in. He stays there, taking in the view. "It's funny. Everything looks so small from here. Makes you realize how big it really is, and how tiny we actually are."

"It isn't always bad to be little," she says. "Just look at me."

He turns around. "You're not that little."

She purses her lips at him. "I'm five foot one."

"Damn. I take it back."

"Well, you know, I came from the countryside. Spent my whole life on a farm. I'm used to being small. Now that I'm here in the middle of all of this… I don't know. It makes me feel like I'm a part of something big, for once. Something actually important."

"So you like it here more than back home?"

"I'm not sure. Nothing ever changed at home. Same faces, same conversations every day. It felt so pointless to me. At least here things happen that mean something."

He smiles. "Milking cows can be important, too."

She shakes her head at him and laughs. "I know you don't actually care, but we never had cows on the farm. Just so you know."

"Aren't cows essential to a farm?"

"Papa didn't think they were worth the effort."

David narrows his eyes. "You had chickens?"

"Oh yeah. Lots and lots of chickens. A few pigs over the years, too. And the two horses."

"Two horses?"

"A boy and a girl."

He puts his tongue in his cheek. "Are they together?"

She looks at him funny. "Together?"

"You know, like a couple," he says.

A laugh. "I like to think so. They fight like they are."

"Why are we having this conversation?"

"Would you like to know their names?"

"Whose names?"

She rolls her eyes. "The horses!"

"The horses have names?"

She throws her arms up in the air. "Of course the horses have names!"

"Well, I don't know. I heard some people don't like to name their animals. Makes it easier to kill them when the time comes."

Her hand goes to her heart. "We would never."

David laughs. "Sorry, no one's killing any horses. I misunderstood, I guess. What are their names?"

"Chuck and Jean," she answers.

David turns away and breaks into a fit of laughter.

Maria's hands go to her hips and she stands there smiling and waiting for him to control himself. "Is that funny to you?"

"No, no," he says, biting his lip. "I like those names."

"Have you ever been on a horse?"

"Surprisingly there's not a lot of them walking around the city."

She laughs. "Is that a no?"

"It's a no."

"That's a real shame. It's a lot of fun once you get good at it."

"I'm sure it is." David goes back to his desk and sits. "Well, I'm sorry Tom isn't in, but you're welcome to wait here if you'd like."

"No, that's all right. He's busy, anyways. I shouldn't be bothering him."

"Was it anything important? I could give him a message, if you'd like," he says.

A sigh. "It can wait. Will you tell him I was here, though?"

David nods, and she turns for the door. The clock reads that it's half past two. He drums his foot against the floor and takes a deep breath. "Maria?"

She stops and looks back with a smile. "Yes?"

He looks at her, his hands now rubbing the back of his neck. "To answer your question, I still do get upset sometimes. I'm making peace with being alone, but I won't say it isn't hard. Of course it's hard. Hard not to miss the idea of it. Having a family is what I wanted for my daughter. But for myself, I knew I couldn't do it."

Her eyes go to her feet. "Can I ask you

something?"

"Sure," he says.

"When was it that you knew? That you wanted to leave her, I mean."

"As soon as I finally let myself actually think about doing it. Leaving, I mean. That's when I knew. When I stopped trying to convince myself that staying was right for me after months of everything being shit."

"Months of shit doesn't sound like much fun," she says.

He half-laughs. "Well, of course they weren't all entirely shit."

She cocks her head, in the way a puppy might. "Just so you know, I'm pretty good at telling when someone's lying. I lie sometimes, too."

He laughs, turning back to face her. "That's not entirely a lie. There were those little moments with my daughter, when she was just learning to talk or run or color. When she started to actually acknowledge me as an actual person. Damn. That's what kept me there so long."

"It's the little moments," she says.

He nods to her. "Like riding a horse for the first time?"

A laugh. "Exactly. Or like making a friend."

David smiles.

She smiles, too. "Tom told me about your daughter a few times. As you can tell, I'm bad with names. What was it?"

"It's Lynn," he tells her. "She's almost six now. It's crazy to me how fast time's gone."

Her eyes light up. "Oh, I love that name. It's my mother's."

"Is that right?"

She laughs. "No, no, I'm kidding. See, I lie sometimes, too."

David laughs, too.

6

An old Beatles record spins in the kitchen, finding its way up the staircase and through the bottom of her door. Something about rainy days. Mommy goes about them with this glossed over, empty gaze that makes Lynn sad herself. The little girl lays on her bed now with one of her eyes closed, the other focused on tracing the cracks on the ceiling with her finger. She's staying out of the way – never quite sure what to do when Mommy gets like this.

Her room is colored wall to wall in light pink, by her request, adorned with shelves of books and stuffed animals and picture frames. She sits on the soft, gray rug that covers the floor. Mommy wanted to rip it up, saying it was too dirty and old to stay in her house, but Lynn had insisted it stay. It's her room, she said, and she wanted it. On her bed is Bear, propped up against a pillow and looking over at her.

"I don't like when Mommy gets like this, Bear," she says to him.

The house was Nana and Grandpa's first. Mommy grew up here, and this had been her room from her very first day alive until the day she moved out to be with Daddy. It's a big house; it needed to be. Mommy has two sisters, and though both have married and wandered far away from home now, they all needed their own space growing up.

When the day came that Mommy left Daddy, initially she had brought Lynn here and the two of them lived alongside Nana and Grandpa. They all coexisted fine, and Lynn liked being near her grandparents. But, they felt the house was much too big for them now that they were older, and decided to move a town or two over to a smaller place. Mommy got this house all to herself, out here away from the city.

"I think I'll color today," Lynn says to herself.

She goes over to her desk to get a piece of paper and a worn-out box of crayons. When she pulls open the top, most of the crayons are shaved down to little stubs of color. Some are missing their tips all together.

Taking the paper and crayons back to the floor, she finds the tan and goes about drawing three circles in the center of the paper. The lowest circle gets long, brown hair now. The circle to the right, a little bit higher, gets a matching hairstyle. She gives the highest of the three short hair, and begins to dot the lower half of circles with stubble.

It's simple here at the old house on the bend in

the road. There are the bird-feeders out front and the array of flowers just below. The reds, yellows, and greens blend together and the grass sways in the gentle passing of a breeze, the stillness disrupted but only for a moment. There are the quaint, brown walls, aging ever so slowly, the years past etched in the cracks of the wood. Perfect solitude. They've stood long enough to see children grow and leave and return with children of their own.

Lynn takes out the pink, blue, and red crayons from the box. She looks over at Bear with a frown. "Why are you making that face at me? It's not my fault he isn't here."

She gives the short, floating head a red dress. Another person coming to life. Next come the hands and then the shoes in pink. Finally, blue eyes and a red smile. The little girl goes about adding all these small details carefully, meticulously, like her mother taught her.

The house will always be this way, though Lynn will not. She'll sprout up, she'll learn and she'll love. She'll lose sometimes, too. Things won't be so simple anymore. For one, she'll move away someday. Every now and then her path will lead her back, then to diverge again. But, she won't always be Nana's little pip, and she'll be too big to sit atop Grandpa's knee.

The adventures, the arguments, the afternoons spent daydreaming under the warm touch of the sun. She'll be shaped by all the experiences that come with growing up, and reflect in herself those that have loved her. Like a quilt stitched together with pieces of all those she has known. The girl will carry with her patience like her mother, her father's humor, Grandpa's walk. She'll share Nana's tenderness, her father's strength, and she'll be kind like her mother always taught her to be.

Though her family may be apart, through her they'll stay together.

She is finishing adding in the clothing of the other two people, a man and a woman. The woman has brown eyes, while the man has blue ones like the little girl's.

Sometimes when Mommy is in a better mood, she'll bring two blank canvases into the living room and they'll paint together. Mommy has always had a love for painting, something she has held onto since her youth. It was the only thing she felt she was any good at. She'll often spend her nights by the window, staring off at the stars as she paints. Brush strokes captivating the distant places her mind has wandered off to. Lost somewhere far off in space. Lynn asked her one night before bed why she worked as a cashier if art is what she truly loved. A tinge of sadness had come over Mommy; she had smiled back, but her eyes were glossed over and directed away from her daughter.

Lynn looks over at Bear. "Look, I miss Daddy, too. I want him here just as much as you. But Mommy doesn't, and she makes the rules."

She draws the sun in the top corner of the paper, thin rays of light spiraling from its center. It overlooks the green grass along the bottom and blends in with the blue sky above. The sun is a bright shade of yellow, of course. She stops now and overlooks her work, scrutinizing it for any missing details. A little girl and her two parents, all smiling together. Satisfied, the crayons all return to their places in the box. The scene complete.

Lynn looks back over at Bear. "It makes me sad, too. Really sad. I hope Daddy's okay by himself. I wouldn't want to be all by myself on Christmas."

She gets up off the floor, the drawing in hand, and goes to her desk to find a tack. She takes one and, with great care, sticks the picture up on her bulletin board. There's hope that comes with having it displayed up there.

7

There is Henry in the mirror with only his left cheek covered by a layer of fluffy, white shaving cream, a dull razor in his hand. And there is a man beside him with thin, brown hair and a brown and orange, checkered tie, bent over splashing water on his face. Another man, wearing polished, black boots, sits in the stall behind them, taking care of business only necessary for him to know. Henry has on a bright yellow polo-shirt –the one Maria lent him at the diner this morning. The pants, black suit pants that are a little tight, are Tom's too, as are the black shoes to match. All of it feels a bit loose on his feeble frame, but it doesn't matter. He quite likes having a change of clothes for once, and he quite likes how he looks. He wishes his mother could see him looking as clean as this.

The man beside him stares at himself in the mirror, drops of water falling from his chin. He smells of cigarette smoke, and not faintly so, either.

Henry looks at the man's reflection, offering a sympathetic smile. "Stressful day?"

"Stressful year, more like," the man answers,

flicking his fingers dry. "Might be the holidays making it worse, though."

Henry pulls at the collar of his shirt. "You know, my father used to say a day without stress wasn't a day worth living."

The man dries his hands with the towel. "He must've been a busy man, then."

"Died of a heart attack, actually," Henry says with a laugh. "It might not've been the best advice, in hindsight."

The man laughs at this, too. "Why might you be shaving in here? Your pipes frozen back at home?"

"Something like that," Henry says. "Let me ask you something, very quickly before you go. I know you're probably busy."

"I've got time," he says.

A grunt comes from the stall behind them.

"This shirt. It's not too big, is it?"

The man laughs. "I wouldn't say too big, no."

"It looks all right, you mean?"

"Yeah, sure," he says, unconvincingly. "It looks all right."

"The yellow isn't too bright, either?"

"I actually like the yellow. It's unique-."

He laughs at that. "I don't do this a lot."

"Do what? Put on a shirt?"

"Go on dates. I haven't had much practice these

past fifteen years."

The man shakes his head. "Sorry but I can't say I have much advice to offer."

"But you've been on a few dates, haven't you?"

"A few," he says. "It's been a few years."

"Is it normal to get terribly nervous?"

"Of course. Every man goes through it. Just be yourself. That's all you've really got."

"Thank you for that."

"I wish you luck," he says. "It's damn cold out there. Take her somewhere warm."

"Good advice," Henry says. The man nods and leaves, and Henry is left now with only the man in the stall behind. "Nice to meet you."

He runs the old razor up and down through the shaving cream, leaving jagged streaks across his face like a zebra. It's quite nice, the feeling of a freshly-shaven face. Much like gently sliding one's palm across a blanket. When he was a boy, his Ma would make him shave off his budding mustache every few days, just as it began to actually show. Every one of his friends became obsessed with the idea of growing a fuzzy thing across their upper lip, as much as they always resembled a dead animal. His mother was right, though. He does look better with a clean face.

The stall door opens and a man with balding

gray hair staggers straight out of the bathroom.

Henry laughs and finishes up the shaving. With the towel by the sink he cleans off the end of the razor, and puts it away in his pocket with the can of shaving cream. One last look in the mirror, giving himself a reassuring smile, and he leaves.

The traffic is at a standstill on the streets, cars upon cars of people headed away for the holidays.

When he was only eight or nine he had run from home down these very streets. At that age he had convinced himself that he was an adult and should be treated as such, granted the freedom to say and get whatever he so pleased. This amused his father to no end, of course. His father would laugh and laugh as his little boy grew more frustrated with each passing moment. Then one day Henry decided enough was enough, fleeing in the early afternoon, as fast as his little legs would carry him. The last straw had been something little, like not getting the candy bar he wanted or something of that sort. Of course to a kid as young as him, a candy bar is more important than all else, priceless and so so sweet. Through the streets he ran, headed for nothing really at all.

He laughs at himself, too, thinking back on it. How naïve he had been.

There's the diner. He stops his stride a good distance from it, taking a last glance down at himself.

Being dressed like this is an unusual thing for him, and he wrings at his hands and curses into the wind as he stands there. Maria had gone through so much trouble to get him ready for this, and he feels obliged to go through with it at this point solely because of the promise he made to her. He remembers now why he told himself he'd never in his life make another promise. How silly he had been getting himself caught up in all this.

The door creaks as he pushes it open. Maria turns to look, smiling instantly at the sight of Henry. She admires how he looks for a moment, her mouth dropping open in awe. Quickly then she makes her way over, nearly running, and grabs a menu for him. "Table for two today, sir?"

Henry gives her a look, which she smiles even wider at. "Might I add, you look quite dapper this morning."

"Thank you," he says shyly.

She leads him over to his usual booth by the window. "Just so you know, *she* sat down about fifteen minutes ago so don't wait around. Her food will be out in just a second or two."

Henry nods, and Maria turns for the kitchen. He's still wringing at his hands, which have become noticeably sweatier since he's been in the diner. A song plays in the background, something soft and peaceful. It does nothing but add to the chaos of his thoughts. He grabs at the menu to make himself look occupied, and stares at it with vacant eyes.

His stomach churns with the same nerves he felt the day he told his father he quit the school baseball team. It wasn't a hard choice because of the sport, but rather a hard choice because his father loved it. Henry never wanted to disappoint him, but he was never much of an athlete and he'd much rather watch than play. The only time he liked to play was with his old man, if it meant they'd be spending that time together. And at first his father had been disappointed, as much as he tried to hide it. But, with all things, his father soon let it go.

Henry hears footsteps coming from behind. Maria passes by with a plate of eggs, over-easy, covered with black pepper. She goes to a table in the center, where the woman sits wearing a gray sweater. Her face brightens at the sight of the food, and she thanks Maria with an elegance Henry can't help but adore. There's something so pure about the way she acts.

Maria comes back to him now, holding her hands out in confusion, looking at him as if he's a child. "Well? What are you waiting for?"

"I'll be honest with you," he whispers back, "I'm beginning to have second thoughts about all this."

A roll of the eyes. "Henry, don't you dare do this to me."

"Do what?"

"I've been looking forward to this all day. You can't chicken out on me now. I'll be crushed."

He squints his eyes at her. "When did this become about you?"

She begins to smile. "That shirt looks good on you, you know."

"Not too yellow?"

"No, just the right amount. Now, are you going to go over there on your own or do I have to do it for you?"

"That doesn't sound so bad," he says.

A shake of the head. "Last chance."

"Maria, I can't."

"Wait here," she says. Her ponytail bobs from side to side as she crosses the diner. Henry can tell she's taking her sweet time, letting him sit in agony, if for nothing else but her own amusement. Only a few feet from the table, she turns back and winks at him. A wry smile spread across her face. He takes a sip of his coffee and scratches at a rash forming on his neck.

He sees Maria bend over close to the woman and smile. A piece of half-eaten toast and its subsequent crumbs lay a waste on the lone plate on the table, and the woman lets Maria take it. He does his best to make his watching less obvious, not that it really matters with no one around to notice.

Then, Maria points her finger. Overzealously, directly, straight at him over at the booth by the windows. Like something straight out of a play, so dramatic and intentional and awful. The woman's eyes go to him, and he quickly looks down at his cold eggs, moving them around his plate a little, his face burning up. This was a mistake, this was a mistake, this was a mistake. He wants nothing more in this moment than to fall through the floor of the diner. He can hear the two of them giggling, surely about him.

He lifts his eyes from the plate just barely, considering it fine to do so, having given up on this pipe dream of his already, uncaring as to what happens now. He sees the woman nodding. Smiling, too, her face overcome by a light shade of red. Maria talks still, and he begins to wonder what it is she could be saying. Surely there isn't that much to say at this point, unless the woman needs convincing to approach him. In that case, he'd rather her not come over to him at all than to come out of guilt.

The woman looks over to him again, and they meet eyes for just a moment. Henry looks away almost immediately, his stomach jumping, spinning, bursting, his eyes going to the wall, out the window, anywhere else but to her, pretending now to watch the cars pass. He hears the screeching of a chair against the floor. He hears approaching footsteps. He hears his own heart in his chest.

"Henry, is it?"

He looks up at her timidly. She is smiling, her cheeks still a rosy shade, her gaze delicate. "Yes, Henry," he answers. "And you are?"

"Eileen. Can I sit?"

"Please," he says.

"That waitress sent me over here," she says, sliding into the booth. "But you know that."

"I figured she might," he says.

"She said I better talk to you."

He looks over at Maria, who acts busy at a table in the corner. "She said that?"

"Well, she said a little more than just that," she says, beginning to blush.

"I really didn't mean for her to bother –"

"It's no bother," she answers. "Really."

Henry rubs his hand along the top of his head. "It was just my thinking that you might like some company. Not to assume anything, of course. What I really should've said was that I'd quite like your company."

"And how do you know that?"

He frowns, puzzled. "How do I know?"

A smile. "Yes. How do you know you'd like my company? We've never talked before. I could be painfully uninteresting, couldn't I?"

"Well, I guess I can't be entirely sure," he says. "But you certainly strike me as a woman I'd like to know."

A gentle smile. "That isn't something you hear much when you get as old as me."

He raises his eyebrows. "Is thirty what they call old nowadays?"

"You're just being sweet now," she says, laughing. "God, the things I'd do to be thirty again."

Henry laughs, too. "We don't appreciate what we've got when we're young, do we? Then suddenly everything starts to hurt like hell just getting out of bed."

"Getting older really is a cruel thing."

"No one really ever tells you how hard it'll be until you get there."

Eileen looks past Henry. "That waitress is a sweet girl. I hope she's enjoying the time she's got being so young."

"She's a real sweet girl. Although she's a little mischievous, too," he says. "Going around saying anything and everything she pleases."

A wider smile this time. "With the best of intentions."

"You're right, you know," he says. "Really she did me a favor. I'm a shy man. Not so shy I won't talk to a woman if I must. But shy enough that I dread it all the same."

"I think you're doing fine so far. I'm not so good at it myself."

"You walked right over here like it was nothing," he tells her.

A shrug. "Everyone has to take a few risks in their life, don't they? Or they won't feel like they've lived very much at all."

"Well, I'd like to take one myself," he says, drumming his fingers against the table. "If you don't mind me doing so."

"I don't mind," she says.

"I'd like to take you out. On a date. Do you mind if I call it that?"

"That's quite all right. I'm not sure what else you'd call it."

"All right, then. We'll call it a date."

"Lovely," she says with a laugh. "And what is it we'll do on this date?"

Henry hesitates. "Well, I've got a few ideas. But, only if you like them, of course."

"Let's hear them, Henry," she says.

"I'd like to take you through the city, like your own tour guide, almost," he begins, unsteadily.

"Although now that I'm saying this it sounds a little silly."

She laughs at his shyness. "I've lived here for almost thirty years now, and I feel like I've seen almost none of it. Where would you be taking me?"

"None of it? Surely that can't be true," he says.

"It is, I'm afraid. I let the time pass me by, it seems," she answers.

"Well, you're in luck, I suppose. I was planning to bring you around to some of the best sights in the city. They're beautiful in their own right, though most people don't ever seem to notice them."

"That'll be lovely. Was it tonight you had in mind?"

"Yes, but only if that works for you," he says.

"It works perfect for me," she says.

"I figure we might meet here, if that suits you."

She laughs. "That'd be fitting, really. I've only known you as the man sitting in this booth staring across at me."

He looks out the window, shaking his head. "And to think, I thought I was being so sneaky about that."

"I quite liked the attention, really," she says.

"You know, Eileen's a real beautiful name. I had a girlfriend named Eileen once. I always say she was the one that got away."

She begins to giggle. "It's funny. The waitress told me you might say that. I didn't believe her."

Henry breaks into laughter, too, his cheeks beginning to flush with pink. "She gave away all my tricks!"

Maria brings over two cups of coffee to the table. She smirks at Henry, and he shakes his head at her. They both thank her, and let quiet come over the table as they sip their steaming drinks.

The morning is shifting into afternoon, the sun almost at its peak and the early cold beginning to soften ever so slightly. Despite this, the diner is still busy with breakfast orders and conversations. Stories being written -- becoming pages, becoming chapters – one word at a time.

8

Tomorrow it is to be Christmas. David looks at the calendar taped to the wall again, just to be sure, running his finger down the 'Wednesday' column until it finds the 25th of December. He slams his hand against it and the calendar falls onto the hardwood.

It's all so goddamn unfair. His father left him, for no good reason, either, but, rather, out of bitter spite born from preconceptions about what's right and what's wrong, although it's all so goddamn twisted; and then, of course, he started to hate his wife on account of her giving him the most cherished thing he has in his life, bringing him into an adulthood that soon sent him spiraling into a confused and desperate paralysis, in which all he wanted was to escape and be young and stupidly drunk, to have an existence not tied down by another person. Yet, with all that spawns Lynn, spawns this part of him that he wants to hold so close, so tight within his arms, to have her with him forever, never to let go, to feel her with him. And, really, in all sincerity he means this, though, truly it does feel all a little twisted. With the one love he has comes this realization that he must live with the choices he has made, and must coexist with a part of him he can't seem to come to terms with. It's all a mess, a headache, persistent, unrelenting, lasting.

So, go on, leave the office, lock the door, go to the stairs. With a sigh, go down the steps, go out the door. Greet the brisk air, welcome it. Breathe in the freshness, light a cigarette, because why not, turn the key, ignite the car. Drive in silence. Watch as the world goes on around. Stop and start with the other cars; give an impression of being ordinary. Dissidence won't be tolerated in a city so mindless. Watch the people cross, their bodies blending together like water colors running together on canvas, stepping in sync along the concrete. None of it makes sense, not that it must as long as time continues to tick. There's no time for being lost, for evaluation, when the days are still constantly moving towards sunset and the racing of traffic churns on, a cruel ebb and flow.

This time last year David spent Christmas Eve behind Lynn on a sled, drawing lines in the snow and feeling like a kid again. Shannon stayed in, saying it was too cold to be out. That didn't bother him much; he preferred having Lynn all to himself. She was afraid of going down the hill at first, and it took a lot of convincing to get her on the sled at all. With his arms wrapped tight around her, he inched them forward with his feet, whispering in her ear that it would be fun. Soon he felt them begin to tip, the sled waning ever so slightly on the edge. Lynn leaned back closer to him, and they lurched forward.

It's a quick drive from the office to home, but today he stops halfway to go to the grocery store. He knows it's better to stop here now than later when the entire city erupts with holiday spirit. Get out of the car, toss the cigarette, go inside. The place is teeming with last minute shoppers, pushing their carts along as if everyone else is in their way, irrefutably pissed off.

He keeps his eyes low by his feet as he makes his way through the herds, trying his best to avoid any conversations about the holidays or any conversations about anything. Take a left, eyes forward, head for the cases of beer. It'll be a long night.

As it turns out, Lynn loved sledding. Once her initial fear, and the screaming, subsided, quickly her terror became ecstasy; the kind only a child feels. They spent the day trudging up and down that hill, stepping into their old footsteps on their way back to the top each time. With each run, she became more and more confident. Eventually, she held out her hand when he went to get on behind her. Daddy, she said, I want to go by myself this time. With great pride in the daughter he was raising, he took a step back and watched her roll away from him. Another memory he would hold dear, throughout it all.

Turn around, beers in hand. Across the aisle is a little boy with messy, blonde hair that juts out in every direction. He tugs at the sleeve of his father's coat, staring up at the man and begging for attention. The father is distracted by all the different brands of cheese to notice right away, but the boy is not to be ignored. He calls up to the man, a look of concern across his face. David stands there clutching his beers and watching. At long last, the father bends down to his son's level with a smile. He listens as the boy talks directly into his ear, pointing off somewhere. After a moment, the man starts to laugh, and leads his son by the hand a few sections down. The boy reaches for a carton of chocolate milk, his face bright with excitement.

David feels heat rush to his face, a feeling of vertigo overwhelming him. His whole body begins to buckle up, the strength leaving his knees all at once. It's all too much for him, seeing the little boy and the father, all these families, the chaos, and it takes all he has not to fall to the floor and lay helpless. He quickly tosses the beers back onto the shelf and stumbles for the exit, his vision slowly losing its focus like a foggy lens. His face a red shade, jaw tight, his eyes low to the floor. Pass the registers, go out the doors, feel the cold.

Breathe.

He falls back against the curb and puts his hands up on his cheeks. People pass by, talking of nothing, stepping around his legs, looking down at him. He doesn't care if he's seen like this. It doesn't matter to him, not at all with everything else going on in his head. The little boy and the father would be together tomorrow. The boy would wake up to a tree surrounded by gifts, lit with white lights and smelling of pine, and the two of them would hug and laugh and be together. The father and the son will make memories they won't soon forget.

David craves a cigarette more than anything else. It's funny, in a way. Around the time he had gone sledding with Lynn was about the time he started smoking. A way to cope with the pangs of disillusion constant in his chest. At a time when he felt so lost with the shape of his life, when Shannon and him could do nothing other than argue, smoking gave him something to hold onto that felt tangible. Something to ease the shaking of his hands.

He hears a soft voice in front of him, and he looks up. Standing over him is a little girl, and she's frowning. Light brown hair curls down her back, and wide eyes stare at David. "What's wrong? Were you crying?"

He shakes his head and tries his best to force a smile. "I'm all right. Just getting old."

She squints at him. "You don't look very old."

"Older than you, at least," he says.

"You can tell me what's actually bothering you, you know. I won't tell anyone else."

A thin smile. "I'm not sure you'd get it."

She crosses her arms. "I'm nine, you know. I'm smarter than you might think."

"I know, I know." For a moment, he says nothing more, staring out at the cars sifting through the lot, putting all his thoughts together. "I'll put it like this for you. Have you ever gotten something you weren't expecting, or you didn't really want? And you knew it wasn't quite right for you? But you still gave it a chance, and you really tried to like it. You know it's not what you want, but you do everything you can to enjoy it. There's that part of you that feels like you should stick with it because you really do want to love it. But deep down you know it wasn't the thing you asked for, and that you couldn't keep pretending. Has that ever happened to you?"

The girl ponders this for a moment, turning her head, much in the way a puppy might. "Do you mean like getting gifts?"

He shrugs, and nods his head. "Sure, you could think of it that way. I got something, and realized I wasn't ready for it."

"My little sister does that. You should see her Christmas list."

A laugh. "Is there a lot on it?"

"So much! I don't know if there's anything left for her to even ask for."

"And what happens?"

"My parents get her as much of it as they can and she barely touches any of it. She'll use everything one or two times, but there's always one toy she loves way more than the rest and she only really plays with that. Everything else ends up with me or put away in the closet."

"I guess that's just how little kids are," David says. "I'm sure I was the same way."

"But that's what I mean," she says, her hands out in front of her, moving as she talks. "Me and you are older now and we actually know what we want. We might only ask for one thing, but it's exactly what we want."

David stares off into the parking lot. "What's your one thing this year?"

"I want an Easy Bake Oven," she says with a proud smile. "I'll be the first girl in my class to get one."

He raises his eyebrows. "Is that right?"

"When I get to be as old as you I'll open my own bakery. I have to start learning somewhere."

"That's a fun dream to have."

"It's really more of a career path," she says. "My mom calls it a dream, too, but if I know it'll come true then really it's more than a dream, right?"

"I guess it would have to be."

"A lot of my friends at school want to be teachers or nurses. Things like that. I'd rather not be dealing with blood or snotty kids like my sister all day."

"I don't blame you," David says. "So you only asked for the oven? Nothing else at all?"

"Well, I put a couple other things on there, too. It's only fair to me if my sister's asking for twenty things."

"You seem like you've got this life thing pretty well figured out," David says.

"My mom says I'm mature for my age," she says. "What's your one thing?"

"My one thing?"

"Yeah. What you want for Christmas."

"I don't really know," he admits. "I'm still thinking."

She cocks her head at him. "You only have one day left to decide, you know."

"I guess I haven't had that much time to think about it."

"I'm selling girl scout cookies," she says, her face lighting up. "Maybe that's what you want."

David smiles. "That's not a bad sales pitch."

"I've been practicing," she says. "So far I've sold the most in my troop."

"How many boxes is that?"

"Seven so far," she says.

David laughs. "Just seven?"

"Well, if you count my mom then fourteen. But don't tell any of the other girls about that."

"I promise," he says. "How much do they go for?"

"Five dollars each."

He squints at her. "That's a little high, don't you think?"

She doesn't flinch. "I have to make a profit, don't I?"

David smiles and leans back on his hands. "It's Christmas time. That's not really the spirit."

A cross of the arms. "Are you going to buy one or not?"

"Make it four each and we've got a deal."

She smiles triumphantly. "Deal."

9

As it turns out, two people over the age of fifty aren't very good at spending a night out. Go back thirty years, pump the youth back into their hearts, bring Henry's hair back to life, and maybe then they'd have the energy. To see the city in the way Henry wants is a lot to do when it's as hectic as it is tonight.

But in his eyes this night couldn't be any better. Plus, he could use the exercise. This gasping of his lungs crying out for air, reminds him of days spent playing baseball with his father. They'd go out to the backyard, gloves in hand, and he'd feel as though he was out in pinstripes for the Yankees. He would run his heart out, until his little legs could no longer muster the energy to push him forward.

Eileen is magnificent company. She wears the red coat, of course, and little, red flats to match. Her hair is tied up in a bun, and she looks beautiful in the quick moments light streaks across her face. Glowing like a jewel in a land of concrete. To have her with him feels like gold; like the sun against his back, like morning coffee. Everything about the day is that of a dream. A hopeful wish made upon the flick of a coin into the sea.

To think he is the fool, the one the people mock and spit on and scold, the one that couldn't make it, now holding the arm of an angel and leading her through crowds of faces unknown in this grand city. It is him, in fact, that sits by the barbershop on Parsons Street and watches with great intent the hurried moving of the crowd. It is him that pulls faces from the tides, and crafts stories about them to pass the time. Giving them identities, if not to forget his own for a moment. For once, however, it's his story playing out on the screen, and he feels a genuine interest in what direction it might go as it unfolds.

They have seen already some of his favorite buildings. The bank that is carved like a palace, its tall columns resembling those in Rome he once read about as a boy. They saw also the stretch of law and accounting and trading firms that split the clouds and fill the lack of trees with their own shadows. Eileen had stood directly beneath one in particular, staring up in childlike awe. She asked him then if he'd ever been to the very top, to which he said no, he hadn't. She said it must feel as though the whole city is your kingdom, to do with it whatever you might like. To this he said that sounded quite nice, but he is deathly afraid of heights and would never dare go up so high by himself.

But then, of course, he brought her to his father's old business. The true pride and joy of his father's life. Boarded up windows, a chain-link fence stretching across the front, the walls chipped and cracked – it hadn't aged well at all. Yet, there is solace to be found in the small patches of green moss, in the wiry arms of budding trees, in the faint remains of the hammer logo on the front. Alive still, despite all that has passed it by.

Back when his father still stood ten feet over him, Henry had come into work one day with him. A memory still so prevalent. The firm hold of his father's hand, the feeling of safety being beside him. All the faces of men that thought of his father as their superior, smiling down at Henry as he is introduced. He had wondered then if his father was some kind of king.

Eileen pulls on his arm. "Could we stop for a little bit, Henry?"

"I think that'd be best," he answers. "But just for the record – it was you that wanted a break. Not me."

She smiles. "Oh, hush. You look like you might keel over any minute."

Henry laughs at this, and they duck into the first place they pass, a small bakery. It's fairly empty considering how busy the world outside it is, lit only by two faint, overhead lights. The place feels like their own little safe haven from all the commotion.

"Even on Christmas Eve you're open this late?" Henry asks the short man with combed, brown hair behind the counter.

"It's the best day of year for business. We better be," he answers.

"Well, we're happy to've found some reprieve from this cold," Henry says. "Two coffees, please."

The man nods and gets to pouring them, and Eileen whispers in Henry's ear: "You really don't need to get me this. I'm all right."

He holds up a hand. "Look at you. You're shivering."

A smile. "I'm old. I'm always shaking."

He chuckles. "Well, a lady like you deserves to be treated. I want to."

The man puts their coffees down on the counter. Henry pulls a bag of change from his pocket, sorts through it, and pays.

Encircling them along the walls are colorless landscapes of city life, and around the paintings there are small signs boasting of the pleasures of sweets. Aromas of coffee beans and cupcakes and pastries come together in this harmonious way only found in daydreams or grandma's oven, and bakeries like this, of course. Follow the smell to the display cases, through the glass see the handcrafted delicacies selling for fifty cents each. Muffins, scones, cannoli, cakes; placed atop thin, shining, white plates that are pristine and lovely.

Henry passes them by as he follows Eileen to a quiet table in the corner of the place. They each sit on a stool, letting the warmth of the coffee breathe welcomed color back into their fingertips and assuage the numbness of their bodies. He takes too quick of a sip and burns the tip of his tongue, but he doesn't mind the feeling much given it's one he hasn't known in years. It brings him a smile, actually.

"This is good," Eileen says. "Just what I needed."

"Coffee makes everything better," he says.

She laughs at him. "I think one of these signs in here says that exact same thing."

"Must be a wise sign, then."

Eileen blows steam away from the brim of her mug. "It's funny, isn't it? I always thought getting older meant getting wiser, but I wouldn't say I'm any smarter than I was ten years ago."

"Wiser in the sense that you've seen more in your life," he says. "I agree that I'm not better at arithmetic now than I ever was. But I know more about life, I think."

"That's an interesting take on it," she says.

"I've seen so many people," he says. "I'm beginning to figure out how they tick. You know, how they think, how to judge their moods."

"I take it you like people watching, then?"

"Don't you? I find it fascinating. We all lead such different lives, and like different things. I bet most of the people I notice have never seen me. And yet here we all are coexisting somehow."

"I'm the opposite, really," she says with a laugh. "After so many years writing for a paper, I've been trained just to focus on the big stories. You know, the ones you'll see in the headlines. There simply isn't enough time to really dig deeper, as sad as that is."

"You write?"

"I do," she says. "Mostly weekly pieces. They aren't about the individuals, unfortunately. They're about the collective city."

"So you still get to tell stories, at least," he says.

"They just aren't my own," she says. "That's wistful of me, I know."

"But you enjoy it, don't you?"

"It's what I wanted out of college. As long as I keep up with it, I know I'll be secure. How could we ever run out of stories?"

He laughs. "It's a job for life, then."

"Exactly, and I know I shouldn't complain about that. I'm so lucky to have stumbled into it."

"I'm sure it wasn't simply luck. You went through school to get there," he says.

"Sure, I did. But it was simply the right timing when I went in to apply. One of their writers finally retired after forty or so years there, and they had the spot open. I stumbled in, fresh out of school and still worried about how the world might treat me."

"And they gave you a home."

"They did," she says. "It was such a blessing."

"But, tell me. What do you wish was different about it?"

"I spend so much time keep tracking of other people's stories. It's never my own. I find myself losing track of how I feel or what I want because I'm too busy with the story for the week. And sure, these stories will keep coming and they'll keep being told. But, it doesn't always have to be me telling them. Just as quickly as the last woman, they can replace me."

"But no one will have the same voice as you," Henry says. "They can't."

"I wonder what my voice actually sounds like. My time will run out, and I'll have spent it on everything but my own life."

Henry gives her a half-smile. "Then I think you know what you have to do. No one can stop you from making that change."

"I'm comfortable, though," she says. "I don't mean to be taking that for granted. It's a job I feel lucky to have."

"I don't mean to be telling you to quit your job and flip your life upside down. But, being comfortable doesn't always mean you're happy. And in the end, that happiness will be the most important thing."

She takes a sip of her coffee. The movement outside flows without interruption. "Routines can be hard to break, can't they?"

"Sure they are. Some days I still wake up worried I've forgotten to water my mother's plants," he says with a laugh. "Besides little chores like that, there never was any need for a routine when we were young."

Eileen smiles. "My sister and I used to spend hours at a time laying on the grass in the backyard. God, what did we even talk about? It didn't matter to us, we were just happy to be outside, under the sun."

"My brother would call me an asshole and I'd say it right back. Most of our conversations went like that."

"You two assholes loved each other more than you'd ever admit, I bet," she says.

"Hell, I'd give anything to hear him say it

again. Even to have him wrestling me to the ground and spitting on me. I wouldn't mind at all."

She laughs. "Boys are weird."

He laughs, too. "Well, we used to think girls were aliens."

"And that we had cooties, too, I imagine."

"My brother would tell me they were sent from space solely to ruin all our fun."

She nods in agreement. "From what you're telling me, your brother seems like a charming guy. And he might've been on to something."

"He was an asshole," Henry says, smiling, his cheeks a faint pink. "The biggest asshole."

10

Maria looks into the mirror hanging on the bedroom door, expressionless. Her hair is tied up in a bun that rests, deflated, at the top of her head. It's late, almost ten by now, and the night has come to full fruition outside. In the apartment, there's nothing but quiet. Tom is out picking up Chinese take-out for a late dinner, both too busy thinking of tomorrow, of Christmas, to bother with cooking anything. The plan is to drive to his childhood home in the morning for lunch and to hers for dinner after.

She sits on their bed, its old springs crying out under her weight. The walls covered in tan wallpaper, barren of any decorations except for a framed *Planet of the Apes* poster he bought last year. The shades are pulled down, and the door is shut. Her hands go to her face, to her eyes, pressing tight. All her willpower going into holding it together; letting her cheeks stay dry, at least for tonight.

Maybe it's homesickness. She does miss the way home felt. Memories lining the wall, encased between the borders of picture frames; quick snapshots preserving those times long past. Light bleeding in through the windows and brightening the old house. It's simple there.

It was nice to have Ma with her, too. It may not have been the right time for here to leave. She can remember the warmth of the oven against her face as Ma made dinner. The flush of Ma's cheeks as she worked. The smells of a finished product, and the prideful smile that came with it. Infectious, pure. A tender collection of memories from those nights spent in their little kitchen, Ma and her.

The cooking only ever began after five o'clock no matter how hungry she claimed to be; any earlier and she'd be asking for more by bedtime, Ma would tell her. Maria still fought her on it.

Ma always made it a production. Meals are special, she'd say, and you must treat them as such. She loved to be dramatic. Every pot would find its way to the counter, every burner brought to a fiery life. The ingredients pulled out of the cabinet by the dozen, or as many as she could fit in her arms all at once. It made no difference what she planned to make – everything had to be out before she could begin. Meats, cheeses, fruits, greens, blues, reds, yellows. The colors all mixing together like chalk drawings in a gentle rain. Some nights as Maria would wonder if there even was a plan. Either Ma was a genius chef, or a master at imitating one.

Ma called Maria her protégé. She never really knew what it meant, yet took pride in the role all the same. She would sit on the other side of the counter, just barely tall enough to see over it, awaiting the final creation.

When Ma would make a dessert, she got to lick the spoon clean of frosting. The smell of fresh butter, the sounds of a whisk churning against the bowl, Ma's smile. The chocolate would always be too bitter, the vanilla too sweet. And Ma would always laugh at her lips, which would inevitably be covered with remnants of brown and white. Sometimes Ma would let Maria take bites of the raw onions she was busy cutting up, their fumes teasing the little girl's eyes into sadness, though she'd be smiling and singing along with Ma. Every now and then she'll give Maria a spoon to lick clean of cookie dough, and they'll giggle together when it inevitably gets all over her lips. Just Ma and her, at a blissful distance away from all else.

Those nights when she would sing were always Maria's favorite. She had a beautiful voice, Ma. So delicate and free. Her voice brought the little kitchen to an energetic life. Songs her mother used to sing to her were now being sung to Maria; a family tree slowly growing roots through the voices of generations past. Maria never got to meet her grandmother, but it's almost like she knows her just a little through her Ma's voice. Sometimes it was Elvis Ma sang, sometimes The Beatles. She'd laugh when she'd start into "Girls Just Wanna Have Fun" with flour all over the countertop, the white powder masking her fingertips and dotting her cheeks. She would hold a whisk to her mouth as a microphone, dancing around with old, paint-stained sweatpants on and her hair tied back. Effortlessly pretty. She'd take Maria's hand and twirl her around the tile floor, passing her love for dancing onto her daughter. Helping Maria learn to love life.

It was a mess, but it was a mess they made together. Just Ma and her, at a blissful distance away from all else.

She drags a black, leather suitcase out from under the bed. The one she had held in the doorway of her old home, Ma crying and Pa sitting in his idling truck. A goodbye she thought had been definite. She pulls a yellow shirt from the closet and folds it up. Into her bag it goes. She hurries, knowing Tom will be home soon. There isn't much; she's never been a girl to own a lot of clothes. A gray sweater, a pair of jeans. The brown flannel she wears on the days she's out in the fields beside her father.

Pa would always spend his nights by the window, staring off at the stars as he painted. He loved painting. The brush strokes captivating the distant places his mind had wandered off to. Lost somewhere far off and foreign to Maria. He once told Maria he often grew tired of this life, tending to the farm and to the animals. Not of his daughter or his wife, her father reassured her, but of the tediousness of it all. Painting gave him some kind of escape from that, Maria thinks. Something like a dream world that offered an escape from here. In the darkness up above was the serene grandeur of places they didn't know.

One night Maria sat by Pa and watched a canvas come to a colorful life, she asked him why he gave up on his dream to work on the farm. And a tinge of sadness had come over her father; he smiled back at her, but his eyes felt emptier, as if stuck somewhere else. "Maria," he had answered, "it was silly of me to think we could live off that. Life is like that. You change when you have to."

"As long as you're happy," she had said.

"I am with you here," he told her.

Maria tried sitting by him that night, to be with him like he wanted. She wanted to keep him company. But she was just a little girl, and her eyes grew weary as the night waned on. Soon all she wanted was to feel the silk of her bedsheets. To let herself drift asleep, and to let her mind wander off to its own dream world. Somewhere far away from there.

Maria pauses. Her hand rests on the soft cloth of her favorite, black dress, and for a moment she finds herself smiling. It's the same dress she wore on her very first date with Tom. Before that, it had been her mother's dress and her father had called it beautiful years ago. Tom told Maria the same thing; that first night with him had felt so precious and surreal. It was the night her eyes first opened to the rest of the world outside her little, red front door in the country. She had felt like she belonged there, in the city, that first night. That she could go out and be a part of it like all the people around her. That she could be more than a farm girl, as much as she holds home so dearly in her heart. There is more to see.

Tom opened her eyes to this new land. He held her hand and guided her along through it all – the alleyways, the skyscrapers, the streetlights. This was her dream world, one she intended to live within. They have been happy together, Tom and her, and this place gives her a feeling she isn't quite ready to part with. After all, Ma taught her never to quit. Girls can be strong, too, Maria.

She begins taking each shirt out of the suitcase one by one. Back onto the hangars, back to how they had been. Things returning to the way they were for the time being.

The day she first moved in she remembers Tom's disbelief at how little she had really brought with her. It made him happy, he had told her. That she wasn't like all the other people in city, with so many outfits they have no idea what to even do with them all. Maria was just the country girl he had always known, simple and sweet, and a girl not willing to let herself slowly become a mirror of all the other faces in the crowd.

The suitcase is zipped closed again, tucked away beneath the bed. Out of sight. For a moment, Maria sits there on the navy-blue comforter and stares at the dresser. Tom loves her, and she knows this to be true. As much as they've been fighting, he has her best intentions in mind. He wants her to become the best that she can be, a trait of his she wants to cherish rather than fight. And she has a friend here that she can't quite come to terms with leaving behind – Henry. The man that listens and jokes and entertains, the man she prays is having the best of nights tonight.

She thinks of Christmas, and how special this year must be for Henry. To have a date and to have a companion after so many years spent alone. She'll be going home and seeing her parents again tomorrow. To her, Christmas will always be found back at home. The quiet streets lost behind the steady cascade of snowflakes. Each flake uniquely chiseled, gently piling into one mass like sparks culminating into an inferno. The lights hung around lamp posts in town square and from glistening tree to glistening tree. Like paintings; the colors, the glow, the energy. All one grand scene taking shape.

The girl from the country goes into the living room, lit only by a lamp in the corner. Her body feels tired all of a sudden, emotionally spent, and she yawns as she drops onto the couch. Its leather is cold against her arms, but she doesn't mind it much. Letting herself relax, letting her thoughts subside, she thinks of nothing. It's like she's breathing for the first time in the last hour, the butterflies finally fleeing her stomach. She can feel her shoulders easing up.

On her tenth Christmas, she gave Ma a bracelet she had weaved at school. Pink string together with blue. Her favorite colors. Maria didn't think it was much. Not nearly enough. Ma's wrist was almost too thick for it to even be worn. Yet her mother had cried and said, Maria, you're all I'll ever need. Then she put on a record, Bob Dylan, and they danced by the warmth of the fireplace just beneath the white tint of the lights around the tree.

She hears footsteps gradually growing louder on the staircase outside. Clicking against the keyhole. The door opens slowly, and Tom pokes his head in. Maria feigns a smile at him from the couch. He pushes it open and holds a bouquet of yellow and white flowers out towards her.

She bites at her lip. "Oh, Tom. Come in, won't you? It must've been freezing out there."

He smiles and brings in a brown paper bag of Chinese food, greasy along the bottom. "For you, my love."

"Look at you being sweet," she says with a laugh.

A shake of the head. "I owe it to you for being such a grouch these last few weeks. Finally we have this little break to be together."

"I think we needed it," she says.

11

To have a woman beside him, absorbing this city as it ripples and changes and loves feels infinitely better than he imagined it would. This city and its people, the stories, oh, all the stories they hold. The most beautiful and complicated collection of stories, rising and falling with the moon, glistening in the streetlights, offering refuge to all those holding dreams bigger than home.

Never has he been much of a romantic, but Henry and Eileen hold hands as they cross the street with a crowd and it feels okay. The collective footsteps are like a drumbeat, each person's breath a wispy cloud of frost in the night. She stands so close that they're touching as they walk, and although it's because of how little space she has more than by choice, he still likes the feeling.

Eileen nudges his arm, a usual smile on her lips, like usual. Her short, gray hair that is usually perfectly in place is a little bit of a mess after all the walking they've done. "Henry?"

He's distracted by the passing apartment buildings, his eyes narrowed as they try to find the numbers on each door. "Yes?"

"Where is it we're headed now?"

He keeps looking off to the side. They pass a bend in the sidewalk and he begins to smile. "You'll see. You're going to love it."

She tugs him out of the way of a pothole in the road, one he wasn't paying the slightest bit of attention to. "You'll hurt yourself before we get there at this rate."

Henry answers with an excited gasp, stopping suddenly against the flow of the night. He looks at Eileen with the same face as a child about to do something they know they really shouldn't. He pulls her by the hand off to their right. Over the curb they go, disbanding away from the pack. Runaways in their own eyes, though the crowd goes on indifferently without them. He leads her into an alleyway, the dull streetlights their only real breadcrumbs along this path.

"I hope you know where this goes," she whispers in his ear.

"It's a shortcut," he says. "I've been coming here since I was a kid. My father would bring me."

The trail of voices behind them softens as they go deeper along their path. Staying close together, they help each other stay balanced as they step over a sewer grate covered in a layer of ice. Shuffling the whole way through the melting snow, the narrow crooks beside them grow darker. The pathway leads them past a dumpster and around to the back of an apartment complex, finally ending at the bottom of a fire escape. Old napkins blow past like tumbleweeds. Cigarette butts lay atop the concrete. They're the only ones around, and there is a haunting silence foreign to this city. Their shoes are so soggy they feel five pounds heavier and their lungs need more air than they can take in, but they've made it.

When Henry's father first brought him and his brother down this alleyway, they were only eight and still believed monsters lived in their closets. Being in such darkness, being led away from the safety of other voices, felt like a cruel trick. His imagination ran wild with monsters hiding around the bend, preying on those that wandered too far. Henry remembers saying a prayer, asking God to spare him. Only days prior, he had skipped Sunday school to play baseball with his friends in the street. Yet, he made a bargain in his head that night, promising that if he lived, he'd stop stealing the five cent laffy-taffy from the candy store and be a better son to his parents. And on and on his father went, leading them into unrelenting blackness, laughing at his two boys as they cried for him to take them home.

Henry stops Eileen at the bottom of a staircase

that winds its way to the stop of the building. "This is it."

Eileen looks at Henry. "And you're sure this is allowed?"

"More or less," he says with a laugh, one that feels unworried and young. "In all my years I've never run into any trouble."

"That doesn't sound foreboding at all," she says.

He smiles at her, taking the first step up with her hand still held in his. She lets her arm stay there, lifted up slightly by his pull, but her feet stay where they are. Looking at him, wondering how all her years of life led her to be here. He stares back. Above them, the stars look down upon the city and offer faint decoration to the already glowing night. Eileen shakes her head and takes the step up, too.

Henry leads her around the spiral staircase, passing the window of a new apartment with each flight they climb. The feeling of emptiness returns to his lungs, but he carries on. If it were to be the last thing he were to do, he would die a happy man. A quick look down and the street is a far beneath them now.

They climb the last set of steps. The rooftop is wet with a thin layer of snow, but it hasn't iced over yet. With the wind snapping at their faces, they pass a jutting vent blowing steam into the sky. Henry can see his own breath dancing from his mouth.

Just a few feet below their shoes, underneath all the brick and mortar, children sleep, spouses kiss, and presents await their unveiling. The night before Christmas, he and his brother used to lay on the floor of the living room and talk of all that Santa would bring. The one day they wanted to fall asleep most, they never could. As being a kid goes.

He takes Eileen to the very edge. The roof is wrapped with a waist-high barrier, and they rest their arms on it.

The view is just as Henry remembers it. White lights for all to see, tangled through the branches of trees and in circles around lampposts. Faces small and indistinguishable coming together as one, a thousand lives crossing paths. Days upon days lived and felt, differing ever so much behind the eyes of each person. Those young and those old, those of wealth and those of struggle. In each of them a book of memories waiting to be penned, their pasts revealed only in the crookedness of their smiles and the depths of their wrinkles. They breathe it in together, Henry and Eileen.

She turns to him, the glistening of distant neon signs dancing in the blacks of her eyes. "And it's only you that knows of this place?"

"Well, now you do, too, I suppose," he says,

smiling. "My father used to bring me and my brother up here every year. Mother used to yell at him that it wasn't safe for us, but he never listened."

"You talk a lot about your father," she says.

"I know," he says. "I think a lot about him, too."

The wind blows past. Henry looks down at his hands, at the redness of his fingers. Though the night is fading, he feels more awake than he has all day. The cold barely bothers him at all now.

"He loved this place. I think he would get so caught up with his work that he never really had time to enjoy life for what it was. Up here, he could have an hour or so of peace and quiet."

"Is that why you come back? To remember those moments with him."

He doesn't answer, choosing not to, and they stand there without words for a few moments. Henry remembers being up on his father's shoulders and feeling as though he ruled the city. A little boy with shaggy, brown hair and the light pull of sleep tugging on his eyelids. So high up, looking down on the tiny, far-off strangers with the gentle sway of his father's breathing keeping him awake. This rooftop their own little kingdom.

Maria squeezes his hand, still smiling up at him ever so lightly. "Would you rather be alone, Henry? I can leave you be for a little while, if you'd like."

"I'd much rather you stay," he says. There's no wavering in his eyes; there's no sadness, no regret. There's only remembrance. Remembrance of times he grew up cherishing, of times he still cherishes so dearly. Of times that shaped him. "I'd much rather not be alone tonight."

She leans against him. "It's nice to know there are still some places we can escape to," she says.

"It does get a little overwhelming. Being here, in all of this," he says, looking out at the skyline.

She nods at this. "I really do think it was the city that kept me from finding a person to be with."

"There isn't much time for someone else. Too much of our time goes to worrying about ourselves first."

"Not after spending a day surrounded by constant people and cars and noise. I get home and all I want is some peace. It never allowed me the energy to get out there."

"Do you regret it, though? Living like you did."

"No, I don't think I can really say I regret it. I'm proud of myself for how hard I've worked. I did achieve a lot with the life I got," she says.

"More than I ever did, surely," he tells her.

She laughs at his kindness, but a sigh comes with it. "But it gets lonely some nights, Henry. It really does."

"Loneliness is a cruel thing," he says. "It should be reserved for men like me only. It only seems fair."

"Men like you?"

"You know, the bums. The guys that couldn't make it."

She puts her hand over his. "Without a man like you, I'd have never felt a night as lovely as this."

Henry smiles now. Unbridled, blissful. He thinks of his childhood; of the bruises, the blisters, the fights with his brother. Of Yankees games with his father, the cursing of the crowd, the ecstasy. Of his mother, the kisses on his forehead, the love, unquestionable and resolute, of the warmth. That time they had together he believed to be everlasting and whole, the only way of life he'd ever have or need. That is the mind of the child, really. To learn what is familiar, growing up with a family he knew as his own, and to think that it'll be forever.

Time, of course, runs out. People change and learn and grow, and people age. They die. He knows this to be true, as hard as it was, and still is, to accept. But at his end, he knows he'll live on in the people he touched. Through all of the stories he was a part of, in the faces he knew, in the friends he made. Through his father and through his mother. His brother. Through Maria and through Eileen. Through the streets and through the city. He knows they are all proud of the man he has become.

For his heart is attached to this city, and a soul never wanders too far from the place it loves.

12

There is a hollowness inside the walls of the house that can be felt in one's soul, a sensation like that of a ghost; devoid of a face but present in the air, nonetheless.

It smells of cigarettes and whiskey. David lays across the leather sofa, staring up at the splinters in the ceiling. He wears nothing but gray sweatpants. A show plays on the TV, the Patty Duke Show, but he's given up trying to follow along. The faces all look too blurred and alike. His mind is busy thinking of other things, anyway. The show is only there to make the house feel a little less empty.

The grandfather clock chimes on the hour. Christmas morning already. The days are starting to blend together. A goddamn long year it's been.

His thoughts wander to his father. To the year he woke up to his father dressed as Santa Claus. David was only nine at the time and he had jumped from his bed screaming in naïve terror, his little arms wrapped close around his chest in fear. His father had laughed and laughed, trying and failing to tell some joke in his panting hysteria. At last, he got out the joke between gasps, saying he had been too drunk to fly the sleigh home the night before. David barely even knew what that meant.

Looking back, that whole scene really was funny to David. And there's a fondness that comes with it; beside the tree that morning he unwrapped the model red Mustang he now keeps on his desk at work. His father had watched his son run it along the hardwood floor, the little, black wheels rolling along with it, and had beamed at the sight of his son's joy. David had looked up at him and smiled, had seen his father's arm around his mother, happiness streaked across both their faces.

In a few months' time, there would be the sound of yelling reverberating through the very same house. David had upset him. A plate would hit the floor, it would smash into pieces, it would drown out his father's voice but only for a second. In the back, there his mother stood. Silent, allowing this to go on. His father always did have a temper, his short fuse ready to light at the gentlest of sparks.

They would always make up in time. They'd go for ice creams in the summer, his father and him. He always got to sit in the front of the car when they went for ice cream. The windows down, the wind whipping against his hair, the smell of fresh mulch. Simple but priceless pleasures. If it was the wintertime, his father would take him to the ice rink.

David never was any good at skating, usually spending more time falling than upright. But, it was time spent with his father. Time when they were both happy being together.

That was the thing about his father. There had always been a kind of bittersweet relationship between them. There were the days when the two of them would be laughing and coexisting and things would seem fine. Content with one another for the time being. It was the expectations his father set that left David drowning. A hellish cycle of never being good enough.

The last time he and his father talked, David refused to sit quietly and listen. He yelled right back. Shannon and him were getting a house, a little one. The one with the oak tree in the backyard. It wasn't much, but they needed a place for the baby and them to be. His father didn't take kindly to any of it, and especially not to the baby. David told him he could handle it, that it was what was best for them. At the time, he truly thought it was. If he was ready to be a man, his father said, then he would be left alone to act like one.

David pulls himself up off the couch with a groan. There's no use in staying up any longer. The television goes dark, and he brings his empty glass into the kitchen. His footsteps reverberate against the floorboards. Out the window, he can see the silhouette of the oak tree in the backyard. Visions of a little girl and of a woman he loves play back through his eyes, their voices and their smiles so pure and present. It's hard to forget days that were once perfect.

Some days did feel perfect; it's true. And some days were full of disdain, brewing from the smallest of disagreements. There were days when they'd kiss each other goodnight and their dreams would be of happy thoughts. Then there were the days when it felt like the fighting might never end. It was him, it always him, that would make her cry those nights. In over their heads, doing their best to stay above the current. Doing their best to raise a child, to figure it all out. Rising and falling with the shifting tide.

Spinning around, he throws the glass across the kitchen at the wall. It shatters into thousands of little pieces, all falling to the floor.

The wind hits against the windows, and the house shudders with it. Echoing the beating within his chest. Deep breaths. His vision like that of a boat struggling to keep itself steady.

He goes to the stairs, fists clenched tight, the hands shaking. Beside him, lined along the wall are the picture frames. One of him as a kid dressed as Elvis for Halloween. Another at the beach, his mother holding his hand in front of the ocean. Him in a hospital bed, barely older than five, the day he got his tonsils out, a tub of vanilla ice cream beside him. Shannon and him smiling on the front steps on their new house; Lynn in her arms, still just a baby. One of him and his father, arms around each other, the day of his high school graduation.

David goes into the bathroom, bending over at the sink. He keeps himself balanced with his hands and stares into the mirror. A reflection he doesn't often acknowledge. Lack of sleep lingers under his eyes. He turns on the sink and splashes the cold water against his skin, letting it shock him back to a reluctant life.

At the back of the sink are Lynn and his toothbrushes, together in a cup. Awaiting her return, and the next time the two of them sang "Here Comes the Sun" together as they brushed – his way of getting her to do it for longer than ten seconds.

This isn't him. Thirty years old; he's not a petulant child that folds at the first thing that goes wrong and wallows in self-pity. Only as a boy could he hide by a light to escape his nightmares. With all things in life came the good and bad. Under the kind light of his memory, searching for happier times in these days of his life that he isn't so happy, the past seems much brighter than really it ever was. The bad times outweighed the good, though now it's easier to recall the good ones only because he has pushed the bad ones out.

Through the times like these, spent in the dark of a quiet house, he'll remember still he's where he needs to be. He made the choices he needed to, and the repercussions of those choices hit harder than he was ready for. But, with growing up comes facing the realities of choices and consequences. Trials and tribulations of a man now alone to his thoughts, accepting it and owning it as his own.

He isn't his father. He's stronger than that. There's no escaping his roots, strong within the ground beneath his feet always. But, there is opportunity to lead a different path, and to shape himself into something better.

"Little darling, it's been a long, cold, lonely winter," David sings out-loud to himself as he goes about brushing his teeth. In the mirror, his reflection smiles back at him.

Made in the USA
Middletown, DE
18 August 2018